6

FILTHY WOLF

A CURVY GIRL AND WOLF SHIFTER ROMANCE

ALPHA WOLVES WANT CURVES

AIDY AWARD

D1603821

FILTHY WOLF

He's lost all control, and only she can soothe his savage beast, until the day she decides to give up that power.

Mik Volkov used to be the Wolf Tzar, now he doesn't even know who or what he is.

He can't shift from his wolf form, and the beast rules his mind, looking for vengeance and violence.

The only thing keeping him sane is his obsession with the woman who smells like ripe peaches and lust.

Key Cross always thought it would be fun to be a psychic, until a wolf bit her and she was cursed with visions she can't control. She wants nothing to do with shifters, until a grumpy wolf who shifts into a hot, naked man whenever she touches him, comes marking his territory by peeing a circle around her.

She belongs to no man or wolf, but they both have a chance to break their curses, and live a normal, boring life again, if they can work together to do the bidding of the Goddess of the Moon. She seems to be doing her very best to play matchmaker with their hearts.

And then came the dragons...

Filthy Wolf continues the adventures of the curvy girls who are more than they seem, and the wolf-shifters who have a thing for marking, claiming, and mating the women who heal their souls. Ahroo!

It also introduces and crosses over into the Dragons Love Curves series for fans of Aidy's whole supernatural world!

For Sean
Digger, Digger?

"The moon does not fight. It attacks no one. It does not worry. It does not try to crush others.

It keeps to its course, but by its very nature, it gently influences. What other body could pull an entire ocean from shore to shore?

The moon is faithful to its nature and its power is never diminished."

— DENG MING-DAO

PROLOGUE

MIK

 eath.
      Despair.
Darkness.

That is all he had known for far too long. Although, he didn't have a good sense of the passage of time. Not since he'd died and been dragged into the Shadow. Not since he'd been killed. Murdered.

Betrayed.

He hid from the rest of the beasts, letting his fur keep him warm, reveling in allowing his tongue to hang out to taste the air, and waiting for his wolf to heal his new wounds. There was power in being only the wolf. His wolf form could fight, hunt, and defend, unlike his weak human flesh. He would never be that powerless, vulnerable man again.

These woods didn't smell right. The trees were too new, the ground too warm, and the small, scurrying animals foreign to his nose.

This wasn't home. But it wasn't a prison like the one his soul had been cast into at his death. He'd learned to use the Shadow when he'd escaped the pits of hell. The monsters that lived below used him as a toy soldier in their coming war, then cast him aside to the Island of the Damned when he'd broken.

But once broken, he felt no more pain. Of course, he also didn't feel pleasure either. His only consuming need now was to destroy those who'd betrayed him.

He'd been close. That woman and her mate had almost led him to the dark one who called himself king.

The wolf he'd become knew what it was to be a king. That word didn't feel quite right in his mind. He'd been no mere ruler on a throne, with a crown. He'd been the alpha of alphas, an emperor, the last hope for his people. The last of the Volkov Wolf Tzars.

If given the chance, he would have been a revolutionary.

He shook his head to toss away the cobwebs of his memory. He shouldn't even have this awareness, consciousness, or remembrances. He was dead. He was nothing.

Not nothing.

My mate.

My savior.

Help me.

The fur on the back of his neck stood up on end. Who had spoken into his head? He narrowed his eyes, scanning the night for signs of demons trying to trick him.

No telltale shadows wavered with their bat-like lizard forms. No minions of evil, then. That was either good or very, very bad. If the Queen of Hell hadn't sent her wyrms after him, it must be either her pawn or her consort.

But no, the voice had been distinctly female. It asked for help from its mate.

A surge of lust rushed through his body, as if his heart was pumping pure need instead of blood. How he would like to take this female and give her more pleasure than she could ever imagine, if only she would submit to him.

He would dominate her, protect her, make her his.

The heat of the desire turned to crystals of ice in his veins. He was no one's mate. Never again would he feel the thrill of having a woman under him. Death did not love, and he was death itself now.

Despite the voice's protest, he was nothing.

In case the voice wasn't a trick by the inhabitants of hell, he opened his mind like he hadn't since he'd been pushed from his former life.

I am not your savior. You must save yourself.

There was no reply to his harsh command, so he closed his mind once again, locking it tight inside the shield of the wolf.

Tonight he would rest, heal, and consider the events of the past few days. He was in this strange foreign land for a reason. He'd scented old friends and foes on the wind and could only hope he'd been given the chance to seek his revenge on those that had betrayed and usurped him.

Tomorrow he would hunt again.

Somewhere not far from his hiding spot, he heard revelers mating under the bright moon. They came together in a sacred spot blessed by the Goddess herself. He wanted to watch, be a voyeur, but that world was no longer his.

He didn't belong there, he didn't belong here, he belonged nowhere.

Nothing.

Another presence shimmered into the darkness. Not a demon, or any other creature of Hell. This one could not contain its light. It sparkled like a million rainbows on the water.

He growled at the intruder. No one was welcome in his presence.

A man, who was achingly familiar, appeared nearby. More than a man, a dragon in his weaker form. He carried old injuries of war that had taken one arm, and he leaned against the tree across from the wolf's hiding spot. He emitted no scent of fear or even caution in the presence of a beast who would happily tear him to shreds and eat him for dinner.

The dragon warrior chuckled and picked at a leaf. "I assure you, pup, I wouldn't taste very good."

Grr.

"I was like you once, you know. Knowing beyond a shadow of a doubt there was nothing in my soul. There was even a girl asking me to save her too."

"Your light is not like my darkness."

"A. That's not my light you're seeing, and B. My darkness faded under the light of love, you douchepotato. I got the girl, and she saved me." His light flickered as if dancing or flying as he spoke of his girl.

"I don't need saving. I am nothing."

Nothing without his power, his control.

"Ah, but we're counting on you to be something. Something very important. Why do you think we dragged you out of Hell?" The last of the man's words faded as he shifted into a great dragon with multi-colored scales.

Fucking dragons.

"I saved you once, pup, but there's someone else you need to find to save yourself this time." The dragon flew over his head and dropped something in the grass in front of him.

A small handheld pastry steamed in the dirt, wafting its scent toward him. He sniffed it and zings of some kind of powerful magic raced from his nose to his cock. The gift from the dragon smelled of ripe peaches and woman.

And he was obsessed.

LONE WOLF SEEKS... PEACHES?

*T*he enforcers for the three powerful packs, here along the coast where Mik roamed as a lone wolf, were brutal in their defense of this territory. They were very good at their jobs.

Mik was better. Better at hunting, better at tracking, better at being an alpha wolf than any of them.

He raised his snout into the air and let the wind fill his senses with all of its secrets. Five wolves tracked him tonight. One whose scent was so familiar it hurt his heart. He wanted to lash out for the pain it caused him. Rip their throats out and watch their blood pool around his paws.

It took all he had every day not to go on the offensive and attack those who kept him on the run and hiding in the shadows. He could rule over them all.

He had.

Before he died.

The enforcers stopped a few feet from the crack in the earth Mik hid in. This area was riddled with shadow-laced entrances to Hell. No wonder the Children of the Goddess of the Moon had been tainted by demons.

Fucking Rasputin.

One by one, the enforces sniffed around the area, searching for his scent. But shadow hid a myriad of sins. Even his.

Being murdered, dragged to Hell and back to life again had some advantages. If that's what being able to sense and use shadow like a fucking demon could be considered.

He'd trade that any day of the week, twice on Sundays, to have his old life and memories back. No, that wasn't exactly right. There was something about his old life that he didn't want. He just couldn't remember what that was. His mind was a jumble of broken thoughts, dream-like images, and pure instinct. The longer he stayed as a wolf, the worse it was getting.

At least he could rely on those animal instincts. His beast mind recognized the frustrated snuffles and snorts of losing the scent of prey, and he settled himself deeper into his hiding spot. Soon enough the enforcers looking for him would run off and report in that he'd evaded them yet again. Then he could return to that which obsessed him.

The reason he was here and wouldn't leave, even if he had to spend most of his time evading the enforcers.

He wouldn't give up hunting her.

Mik locked down his mind, forcing himself not to command these wolves to go, leave him alone. He was no longer their alpha and wouldn't have the ability to bend them to his will anyway. But he wanted to. He needed that control.

The shimmer of the Goddess's magic and the cracking bones as the alpha shifted, crackled across his own fur. The human part of him ached to join them, to stretch his arms, face up to the moonlight, and let it bathe his naked skin. That wasn't happening. Not tonight, not for a thousand nights. Not as long as he was being punished for his misdeeds against her children.

Nikolai Pyotrovich Troika stood up in his human form and commanded the others as Mik had once done. "Shift, brothers. We've lost the bastard's trail again, and I want to know why."

Yes, he knew his pursuer.

This was one memory that, as much as he wished it to be gone, wouldn't stray from the front of his mind. Once upon a time, they'd been friends, brothers in arms, more even. There was no one he'd trusted more with his life than Niko.

That was a mistake he wouldn't make again. And someday soon, Niko would pay for his betrayal.

Even if the other wolves hadn't wanted to shift, they had to do as Niko commanded. No child of the Goddess could disobey a direct order from the Wolf Tzar. Unless, of course, they were under the influence a demon. He and

Niko had learned that the hard way. The very, very, deadly hard way.

Niko's brothers and their pack enforcers joined him in the moonlight, forming a loose circle, their backs to any danger. No creature of the forest would dare attack these masters of their domain. Mik could though.

"I don't like that he can fucking disappear when we're moments from getting to him."

Yes. He could attack them now with their guard down. Five against one wasn't great odds, but he had been trained by the elite Volkov guard to be a warrior. Although so had Niko, and that hadn't helped either of them in the last battle for their lives. Still, he had the element of surprise, and the fact that he was bigger than any of them in his wolf form.

"You're sure it's him?" Niko's youngest brother, Kosta, would be the one to question his alpha. Always so curious, so rebellious, yet loyal to a fault.

It irritated Mik that he could remember details like that, but not how he'd ended up in their territory in the first place.

Niko stared into the forest, and Mik swore those amber eyes were boring straight into his soul. "I don't know how, but yes, I'm sure. It's Mik."

The hair on Mik's scruff stood up on end and every cell in his fur, fangs, claws, and paws went on high alert. Niko knew he was alive.

They should both be dead. How was it that Niko was now the Wolf Tzar, living his best god-damned life, mated, and stalking him? Being dead, passing through the shadow to Hell had done things to Mik's mind, taken his memories and jumbled them up, hid them away in corners of his mind for him to find later.

He remembered the two of them battling ferociously, but not against each other. Someone else, dark and evil, wanted to take Mik's power for their own. Then Mik was dead. Niko had killed him... or... he clenched his jaw and concentrated on the gap in his memory.

Niko died too? No. Here he stood, now surrounded by his pack, his family, and commanding them all with the power that only the Wolf Tzar could yield.

Niko had taken his power, his control, his life.

And Mik was forced to hide in the dirt, living life as a beast, relegated to scraps of his former existence. Had the shadow tainted even the memories he thought were true? A growl bubbled in his throat, and he had to forcibly swallow it down.

Kosta shook his head and leaned against a tree as if challenging his alpha was no big deal. "Nah, it has to be trick. Something the fucking one-bloods are doing to distract you from whatever the hell it is they're planning."

"You forget how he fought against them when Aleksei was being pulled into the shadow." Max was much more respectful in his dissent. Perhaps he should have been by Mik's side that night.

"Fucking Volkovs." Kosta spit on the ground, and a beetle went scurrying into the underbrush. "But if you're sure it's Mik, what the fuck? He's supposed to be dead."

"Yeah, well, so was I." Niko looked again into the forest where Mik was hiding. "Something saved us, thank the Goddess."

Niko had never been all that religious. Neither had Mik. The Goddess was real, but she sure as shit hadn't been around for the past few millennia. It wasn't like she deserved gratitude for anything that happened after she gave her people the gift of the beast inside.

Where was she when his corrupt council had lulled him into believing all was well? When he'd prayed for her guidance to bring wolfkind out of the darkness? When he was fighting for her people?

Where was the Goddess of the Moon when he was being dragged to Hell, begging to be saved? Sure, she existed, but she wasn't worthy of any thanks or praise, because she didn't give a shit about her so-called children.

"So, what do you want to do, our great and powerful alpha?" There went Kosta with that smart mouth again. If the Goddess should forsake anyone, it was this douchepotato.

Where the hell had that thought even come from? Douchepotato was new to his vocabulary. He must have heard it from someone here in the Troika's town.

"I'd say we leave our enforcers here where we lost the trail, but that hasn't done us a bit of good in tracking him down in the past. He's too well trained, and one sneaky son of a Goddess." Niko lifted his face to the moon and closed his eyes, drinking in her light. The magic of the shift shimmered across his skin like silver and gold dust.

"Just spread the word to keep everyone's senses alert and notify me of even the slightest inkling that he's shown himself."

Niko shifted and let out a long, mournful howl. The others did the same, and it was almost more than Mik could bear. Wolves weren't meant to live in solitude. His bones ached to join this pack. They used to be almost like family.

Family who betrayed him for their own gain.

Once Mik figured out how to break this curse holding him in his wolf form, and hunted down those who'd stolen his last life, he would start his own pack.

The other wolves ran off in the various directions of their homes. Mik had silently stalked each of the alphas in this territory and knew where they lived. Niko had the farthest to go to get back home, yet he remained behind. He let out one more howl, that was met by not just the enforcers who'd left, but more wolves from many packs. No way the humans didn't fear that sound resonating up and down the coast.

When the final bray waned, Niko lowered his head. *"I know you're out there, Mikhail Nikolaevich Volkov. Don't hide from me for much longer. I will help you adjust to this new world."*

Good try, Niko. He wasn't drawing Mik out that easily.

But if he wanted to, as the Wolf Tzar, Niko should be able to command Mik to come out. He was able to make his wolfspeak heard in Mik's mind, but hadn't used the ultimate alpha voice to his will. He had the power, yet didn't wield it.

Very suspicious.

Mik curled his claws into the dirt and stone beneath him, anchoring himself to the ground to wait. Niko finally ran off, and Mik wanted to follow him, confront his old friend, and make him admit everything. But he had other plans for tonight that had already been interrupted by this little game of chase.

When the scent of the alphas faded, he crawled back out of the shadowy crack in the earth and stalked toward town. A new aroma filled his senses, replacing the pure masculine energy with someone much more obsession worthy.

She was drenched in the sweet smells of fruit, vanilla, butter, and flour, and strangely, money. Through it all, Mik's body reacted with a fierce desire to the core of her being. Through the rest, she was the ripest of peaches, and he wanted to rip her apart.

Or eat her up.

Or fuck her.

He gave his head a good shake. The base instincts of the beast jumbled together and blended all his wants and needs into a confusing entanglement of obsession. All he knew was that it would become clear once she was his., and he would claim her in whatever way he wanted.

Mark.

Claim.

Mate.

Mate? No, no, no, no, no. He didn't want or need a mate. A pack, yes. A mate? Absolutely not. He was the last of the Volkov line, and it would stay that way. Didn't mean this woman wasn't his.

Mik crept through the dark, sticking to the routes he'd followed a hundred times through the town at night. They all led to the same place. The shop in the center that smelled like her. It was also covered with the scent of every wolf pack member in the wider area, especially the alphas.

He would take the risk if it meant he could watch her.

The moon was high in the sky and the hour late, or early, depending on your perspective. She would be closing the shop soon, and if it was a lonely night, he would have his chance to capture her.

A trash can in the alley across the street that smelled of human urine and food waste hid his own scent from the unsuspecting wolves coming and going. He rolled around on the ground beneath it to saturate his fur with the stench, and then settled in to wait.

She was visible through the windows and a bone deep shiver ran through his body as he watched her. She interacted with her customers, a bright smile on her face that he wanted to wipe away for all its fake happiness. He would rather fuck that mouth until she couldn't breathe rather than see her insipid cheerfulness.

He reveled in that fantasy until that smile dropped and her eyes went from colorful and sparkling to a dull pure white. Her slack, lifeless mouth moved, saying words that even with his wolf's amped up hearing, he couldn't catch. What he got instead of simple observation was the mirrored sensations of his curvy little witch, and that's why he was here.

When her prophetic visions overtook her, the two of them were connected all the way to their very souls.

Her lungs locked. His chest squeezed, searching for breath. The muscles in her stomach clenched. His did the same. Most importantly, her mind went crystal clear, her focus sharp and intense. She saw everything about the person standing in front of her.

Mik's own mind found clarity in that moment too. He didn't give a fuck about the future she saw for the lonely woman standing across the counter from her. Who cared that the human's mate was waiting for her in the bar below? What Mik cared about was that his witch looked at him and had one of her visions.

She was the key to breaking his curse.

Once that was done, then he could fuck her, or kill her. Whichever he wanted. Once she and her visions showed him how to free his mind and body from the beast and its will, he'd be in control again.

His mouth watered with all the ways he would command his world once again. Starting with her.

SON OF A WITCH

ey blinked once, twice, a hundred and fifty-seven more times to clear the brain cloud roiling through her mind. Everyone always thinks it would be so damn cool to be psychic, but no one tells you it's going to ruin your life.

"Well, I never. What an awful thing to say." The woman, holding the other end of a hot hand-held apple pie, yanked the tasty treat away from Key and took an angry bite. She didn't bother to finish chewing and swallowing before she laid into Key, going into full-on rant mode. "I would like to speak to your manager, and you'd better believe I am demanding that this pie be gratis for my trouble."

Wouldn't be the first pie Key had given away because her brain went wackadoodle, and it wouldn't be the last. "I am the manager, and I apologize for whatever it is that I said."

It's not like she could help what came out of her mouth when one of the visions gripped her in its psychic vice.

"That is not acceptable," the angry woman said, with crumbs avalanching out of her mouth.

Key couldn't exactly explain to Ranter Mcrantypants that she was cursed with precognition when an asshole of a wolf shifter had bitten her, which is why she'd said something that hurt Ranty's fragile fucking feelings so much she had to emotional eat her entire pie in fourteen seconds flat.

This lady didn't know the supernatural even existed, and Key wished once again that she didn't either. But, what was done was done, and there was no sense crying over spilled pie. "You know what always fixes me when something shitty happens in my day?"

That was not what Ranty expected to hear. She jerked her head back until her chin melded with her neck and sneered.

"Free pie." Key grabbed a half dozen assorted hand pies with the tongs and slid them into a box. Then she grabbed a couple of coupons for the Sleepy Folk Speakeasy downstairs and slipped them on top, before closing the lid and coming around the counter with the bribe. "Also, a good stiff drink. I'm pretty fond of Galyna's chocolate martinis. They've gotten me through some tough times, you know? Try dipping the chocolate creme pie into the martini. It's damn near magical."

She shoved the box into Ranty's hands and wrapped an arm around her shoulders to help guide her disgruntled customer to the stairs that led down to the bar. "Okay, have fun tonight, and if my fix doesn't solve your problems, come on back and we'll try another combo. Peach pie with a nice dry champagne ought to cure any blues. See you later."

Ranty tilted her head to the side like she was going to say something, but probably for the first time in her life, kept quiet. She continued on down the stairs where she could either fulfill her destiny bestowed upon her by Key's psychic prediction, or be Harley, the bartender's, problem.

"She didn't even know what hit her. How do you do that? Any other cashier would have melted under Mrs. McRaskill's ire." Poppy, a faithful friend and pie shop patron, shook her head and grinned. "Don't tell, but sometimes I hide in the kid's section when she shows up to the library. I know I'm supposed to help everyone looking for a book and shouldn't avoid her, but I can't help it."

Key gave a simple shrug. People were easy. They just wanted to know that life wasn't biting them in the ass all the time. "Pie makes everyone feel better."

It was why she took this job at the Sleepy Folk pie shop in the first place. Way, way better than the county sheriff's office. Never again would she even walk into that building. Nope.

It wasn't like she could hold down any kind of full-time career now anyway. Not with her... condition. "What did I say to that lady anyway?"

Not everyone in town knew about the supernatural beings they were all neighbors with, or Key's consequences from being bitten by one. Poppy was one of those lucky enough to have found a fated mate among the wolf shifters. Key wasn't jealous about that. Not even a little bit. She was so very happy for her friend. So happy.

Of course, when Poppy was marked with a wolf's bite, she hadn't ended up with a special power that had taken over her life. Nope, she'd gotten a super-hot boy toy who worshipped the ground she walked on, and the ability to turn into a wolf.

"Something about whiskey being the love of her life. I think she thought you were calling her an alcoholic." Poppy raised her eyebrows and rolled her eyes in the direction Ranty had retreated.

"Well, we all self-medicate in one way or another to cope, don't we?" She had no idea what the premonition meant. She never did, no matter how many times someone asked.

Key touched the permanent bite mark on her shoulder, wishing it away, and then shook her head at herself. It had been more than a year, and she'd vowed not to let that particular trauma ruin her life any more than it already had. That included feeling like a sad sack.

"Come on. Since I gave cranky-pants a half dozen, it's time to put more into the oven before the late night crowd shows up wanting their ticket to the speakeasy. I'll let you pick the flavor."

"Ooh. Yes, please. Harley loves when I smell like the vanilla cream with chocolate glaze." Poppy got a sort of glazed look herself. "Good times, good times."

Key would tell Poppy exactly how weird and gross she and Harley were, but that was just the little green monster of jealousy talking. "Vanilla with chocolate it is."

Good thing she put those extra pies in the oven, because the next few hours were rocking with customers. Thankfully, no one else spurred one of Key's episodes either. One a night was more than enough for her. But her visions had been more frequent than ever. Since about Thanksgiving, she'd had dozens and dozens. Where before it was maybe one a month or so.

The clock finally struck two, and she yawned. Closing time. Finally. She grabbed the last two remaining pies, a cherry and a peach, and threw them into a paper to-go bag. Those and a cup of coffee would make a great break-fast in a few hours.

Max Troika, the owner and her long ago savior, popped up from downstairs just as Key was closing out the cash register. "We're shooing the last few people out of Sleepy Folk now. You wanna wait a minute and I'll walk you home?"

If Max wasn't her boss, mated and married, and the wolf who'd helped to save her from the horrible former sheriff and his human trafficking plans, she'd have a crush on him. All the Troika boys were extra sexylicious.

But just thinking about how any wolf shifter would want to put their own mark on her, and any feelings of lust went pthththth.

"Nah, that's okay. It's not like there's any wolves in the Reserve that are going to bite me, or anything." There were, in fact, a lot of wolves in the open space area, because that's where they all went to blow off steam after working their day jobs or whatever it was that Max and Galyna had their pack doing all day. It's just that not a one of them would come within two feet of her on orders from their alphas.

That didn't make it hard to find a date at all.

Max gave her an I'm-the-alpha eyebrow raise and tipped his head to the side like an overprotective dog trying to figure out why she was acting stupid. "Good try, Key. It's me or Gal. Your choice. No walking home after dark by yourself."

She was grateful the Troikas did everything they could all day every day to keep her safe. She. Was. "How about Poppy?"

Harley's voice floated up the stairs. "Poppy is indisposed at the moment."

Ew. That meant the two of them were about to go have sex in the keg room. They couldn't keep their hands off each other.

Galyna appeared behind Max and wrapped her arms around him and gave him a peck on the neck. "I volunteer as tribute. I think Key may need some girls only talk."

Gal hadn't developed psychic abilities when she'd

mated with Max, but she was far too perceptive. Key rubbed her palms together and intertwined her fingers, stretching and cracking the joints. "Yeah. Sure. Thanks."

She was trained in self-defense from her time at the sheriff's office, and she didn't really want company on her walk home, but there had been that lone wolf around town at Thanksgiving, so she would just grin and bear it. "I'll meet you out front in five."

With the money put away in the safe for tomorrow's deposit, and the leftover pies in her bag, Key locked the front door, and leaned against the building to wait for Galyna. The night was bright because of the full moon, and she closed her eyes for a moment, just letting the cool and the rays soak in. The lovely night was tainted just a little by the scent of garbage wafting from the dumpster across the street. She glared at it.

Sparkles of light, similar to snowy static on a TV shimmered behind her eyelids, and all her thoughts disintegrated. Nausea roiled around in her gut. All she could do was wait the feeling out and hope no one else was around to witness her Oracle at Delphi impression.

An eternity later, and a hand squeezed her arm. She forced her eyes open to see Gal with her mouth wide open and that look everyone had when Key spewed out a prophecy or whatever the hell it was her mouth did while she was in la-la land. "Sorry, Gal."

"No, no. Don't apologize. I get it. That was just... I mean, no one but Max and our families know yet."

Galyna released Key's arm and pressed a hand to her belly.

"You understood what I said?"

Two visions in one night? That had never happened before. At least this one seemed to be for something nice that was going to happen. Because while Key may not know what she'd said to Gal, it definitely had something to do with her being preggo.

"I hope it wasn't anything to upset you."

Gal shook her head, but her eyes were still moving back and forth as if she was searching around in her brain for an answer to whatever problem Key had given her. She pointed in the direction they needed to walk to get Key home, and started off. "No, it wasn't ominous or anything. Just weird. Two golden dragonlings, plus two Troika wolf pups, equals overnight success for the sacrifice and the savior."

Okay, that was one of her weirder ones. "I do seem to talk about dragons a lot, don't I?"

"More than the average person, yes." As they approached the path that went through the Reserve, Gal paused, sniffed the air, and then looked down at Key's bag. "You wouldn't deny a pregnant lady one of those pies, would you?"

Key laughed and reached into her bag. "Cherry or peach?"

"Cherry for sure." Gal took the proffered treat and ate it in three bites. Unlike Ranty, there was nary a crumb that escaped. Gal looked at the bag again, and Key immediately reached back in and pulled out the peach pie for her too.

"Sorry. I hope this wasn't your dinner. But luckily we own a pie shop because this little guy or girl really likes pie. "

"Who doesn't?" Key wasn't saying she'd gained ten pounds when she first started working at Sleepy Folk Pie Shop, but she wasn't saying she didn't. She didn't mind. The pies were worth it, and it was a good excuse to throw out all of her old clothes from her life before and buy new stuff.

She jerked her chin toward her house. "Okay, here's me."

"Yes, and I will walk you all the way to the door, Kiara Cross. You're my pack, and we take care of our own." Gal's eyes glowed with the pretty blue light of a Troika and Grimm pack wolf. Her voice carried some extra weight that only alphas had.

Key rolled her eyes and stuck out her tongue at her alpha. "Fine. It just seems a waste. My door is right there, and the entire rest of the neighborhood is asleep."

"You know it's not the humans we're worried about."

"Like any wolf will even come near me. My whole yard smells like a dog kennel." Key would continue to happily pretend that she didn't know the one-bloods still had followers who probably wanted her or wanted her dead. They hadn't caused any trouble in months. Not since that lone wolf had scared them off.

A special shiver flittered down her chest and into her

lower belly. She ignored that feeling all together. It happened every time she thought about that very dangerous wolf, and she didn't want to feel that way about any man or beast.

The only thing that would keep her happy was her ordinary life in this quiet neighborhood where everything was nice and boring. She'd had more than enough adventure for one lifetime.

Gal didn't give up for even a second, and she walked Key all the way to her door, even pulling the barred screen door open, waiting for Key to unlock, get in, and reset her alarm system to the home setting. Only then did Gal shift into her pretty dark brown wolf and trotted away into the night.

Key took a long deep breath and let it out on the count of ten. This night was a doozy and all she wanted was to put on her pajamas and have a drink. So that's what she did.

The night was cool, but not chilly, so she put on her flannel pjs, made a Bailey's and hot chocolate, and dragged a blanket out to her lawn chair. She cozied up and took a long, slow sip of the hot drink, and relaxed for the first time in what felt like days.

The moon was so bright tonight, and its light practically made the trees and bushes along the fence glow. Whoa, wait a minute. That big bushy thing fifty feet in front of her that definitely had a glow about it, was not in fact, a bush. She could tell because it just blinked at her.

Eek. And bared its teeth.

Okay. Not good. Bushmaster was a big ass wolf. Biggest one she'd ever seen, and he was coming this way. Slowly, stalking her. So, why wasn't she getting up and running inside?

Come on legs, go. Go, go, go. Nothing. She was glued to her chair. Key shrunk down into the blanket, doing her best impression of a pillow.

"Nice wolfy, wolfy. Go on back to the Reserve now. Shoo. Shoo-shoo." Those words all came out on a quiet rasp, sounding more like Titanic Kate's frozen vocal chords after being stranded for hours on a door that definitely had room for two.

"Why do you glow in the moonlight, my witch? Are you connected to the Goddess?" The deep menacing voice poured into her mind like smoke, and whiskey, and molasses so thick and dark she could drown in it.

"I'm not a witch," she whispered.

The wolf stopped and tipped its head to the side in the adorable way puppies did when they were trying to figure you out. Except he was no puppy. He lowered his head and a warning growl rumbled out of him.

"Oh, was I not supposed to answer that question? My bad. Pretend I didn't say anything."

The wolf stalked closer and growled louder, yet for some stupid reason, just like before, Key's flight or fight response chose freeze instead. Unless someone came along, like a Troika, she was either going to die or be dragged away as captured prey.

It got right up in her face, and the glow around him

was so bright, she had to squint. She turned her head to the side and scrunched one eye shut, waiting for the adrenaline to kick in and do something for her. She didn't want to die.

Except... her heart wasn't pounding, her breathing was normal, and there was no bitter taste of bile in the back of her throat like there should be knowing she was about to die. Huh. Maybe she was already dead and that's why she felt so calm?

The wolf poked his face right into her blankets and snuffled around, getting a little too close to her boobs through the blanket. Inappropriate.

Finally unfreezing, she reached out and smacked the wolf right on the snout. "Bad wolf. Those are my lady parts and not for you to doggy-style motorboat."

The moment she touched the soft fur on his face, the wolf was gone, and a frickin' naked ass movie star, still glowing like he was in the spotlight, poofed into existence in front of her.

Ahem... make that a porn star.

THE MAGIC TOUCH

*O*ne minute he was a beast ready to drag this deliciously plump witch off to the woods, and the next he was back in his human form for the first time since his death.

What. The. Fuck.

He hadn't shifted. There was no breaking and reforming of bones, no splitting of his fur, nothing of the pain that normally came with the shift. He stood there for a moment taking inventory of his own body. It was so unfamiliar, he hardly knew how to use it.

He stretched his neck, turning his head side to side, then noticed the cool night air on his arms, back, legs, and cock.

Well, well, well, at least he knew his cock still had life in it. It was stiff and pointing right toward the object of its desire. Mik fisted it and stared down at the wide eyes of the witch who'd used her powers to break his curse so very easily.

That meant he was free to do with her as he pleased. Just as soon as he found her under the mountain of blankets she'd surrounded herself with. All he could see was her face from her nose up. But he'd felt the lush softness of an ample body under there and he was anxious to get her under him.

He took a step closer, and she squeaked like a little field mouse waiting to be gobbled up. That lightning-fast hand that she'd wielded her spell with popped out of a mysterious fold of the blanket and pointed at his cock. Mik turned to the side so as to deflect any magic she might try on him.

"You put that thing away this instant." She flicked her wrist about and pointed her finger, but no magic sparked from her.

"Where exactly do you expect me to put it?" He was naked, and his cock was rather large.

"Can't you just, like, tuck it away? Do you have to... do that with it?"

"This?" He grinned and gave himself a long hard stroke from base to tip and back again. Mmm. Yes, he wanted to be nice and hard for when he fucked her. He'd start with that gorgeous mouth, and then—

His thoughts stuttered and almost as instantaneously as before, his curse overtook her magic and he shifted, and was once again a wolf. Dammit. What kind of game was this witch playing? Just how powerful was she that she could take and give this kind of curse with such ease? She hadn't even spoken any spell or anything this time.

"Oh. Thank you. That works." His witch sat up straighter and the blankets fell down around her elbows. She wore only a light shift, and even through the material, her skin was alight. No wonder she covered herself so thoroughly when she was out here in plain sight of the world.

Although, the alpha wolftress that had walked home with her didn't even seem to notice the light shining from her exposed hands and head. Then again, she hadn't noticed him trailing them so closely either.

"Shift me back immediately."

"Me? You shift, you're the wolf shifter. It's right there in the name." She lifted a mug from under the blanket and waved it around in his direction, sloshing the contents erratically. The scent of her shifted from pure ripe peaches to a slightly bitter aroma of irritation.

Why the fuck wasn't she scared to death of him? He was a fucking frightening wolf who could eat her up in three to five bites. Probably five because he'd spend a long time savoring those hips, thighs, and ass. Delicious. He moved closer, reveling in her scent and her light, ready to snap her up.

But he couldn't fulfill any of his dark fantasies with her until he was free, and she easily held that power. *"Lift the curse."*

Her brow formed a crinkle, and she narrowed her

31

eyes, studying him. "What are you talking about? Also, why and how are you talking in my head?"

"Because I am—" He was about to say he was the Wolf Tzar and he could speak to anyone, but that wasn't true. He wasn't, and only the ultimate alpha had that power. "I am a powerful alpha, and you are mine."

"I'm your what?" She asked that as a genuine question.

This woman had the scent of a dozen wolves, including all the alphas in this area, surrounding her and her home. She was clearly a valuable member of their society. How could she not understand his claim on her?

And he was claiming her. Perhaps not in the way one would a mate, because he had no room in his life for that kind of relationship, nor did he want one. Regardless, she belonged to him, and he would take her away from the Troikas forever.

Mik pushed his face so close to hers, he could taste the flavor of her skin. His mouth watered with the need to bite her. Just there in soft part between her neck and shoulder. He drew in a breath and recoiled at the scent of another wolf. She was marked.

He growled, darkness tunneling his vision, and the beast rising up to take over his mind. *"You belong to me."*

Instead of cowing, whimpering, and bending to his rage and will, the witch poured her hot beverage over his head. He yelped like a wounded puppy, not because it hurt, it was barely warm enough, but because it startled the shit out of him.

She threw off her blanket, rising up out of the chair,

shining brighter than the moon in the sky. If she wasn't the Goddess herself, she certainly was an acolyte of the moon, a priestess of Ningal. With her hair blowing in the wind, she pointed at him and yelled for all the night to hear. "I belong to no man or wolf. So you can fuck right off with that bullshit."

Mik's bones resonated with the sound of her voice declaring her independence, and he lifted his head and howled at the moon, as if she'd commanded him to join in her cry. Then the strangest thing in his entire existence happened.

His tail wagged.

He had absolutely no control over it, and it wouldn't fucking stop. He wasn't happy. He was angry, and filled with the need for vengeance. If he didn't know he would look like an absolute fool, he'd spin and bite the offending appendage right off.

"And another thing, you asshat in wolf's clothing. Stop. Glowing. You're going to wake the whole neighborhood." She stomped her foot and glared at him.

He wasn't glowing. She was. It made him want to lick her from head to toe and back again. His tail beat the air even faster at that thought. Dammit. Dammit all to Hell. What was this witch doing to him? She was much more powerful than he'd anticipated, and he would not underestimate her again.

Tail still going ballistic, he lowered his head and growled, although not as forcefully as he wanted. *"Stop working your magic on me. I've had everything in my life stripped from me, been to Hell and back, and fought demons more powerful than you to be here. You will do as I say and break this curse with no more of your games."*

Her mouth went slack and silent, and for a moment, he couldn't tell if she was obeying him as she should, or if she was simply mesmerized by the back and forth swishing of his god damned tail.

She dropped her chin to her chest and sighed. The sound irritated him. He liked it better when she fought his fire with her own. "You're exhausting. I'm going to bed. Don't pee in my yard."

She turned and reached for the barred screen door leading to her home. Mik lifted his leg and let a hot stream of urine hit the small cement slab of her back porch.

She spun back around, and her gaze flicked between the mess and his face. "Dude. What the fuck?"

He was about out but pushed two more squirts for good measure. "*Marking my territory.*"

"Marking your territory? Marking your... I'm gonna mark your territory." She marched over to a hose connected to a spigot in the wall and turned it on, then pointed the sprayer to the cement.

Before she could push the button to let loose with the water, Mik pounced on the green coil and stepped on the portion of the hose closest to the ground, squashing it so that when she pointed the nozzle, only a dribble came out of the end.

That sent his tail into another frenzy and this time, his

tongue popped right out of his mouth and lolled out the side.

"Are you... smiling?"

Was he? No. Of course not. He was catching some cool air in his mouth to compensate for the heat coursing through his body because of her.

Because of his rage and anger and lust for her.

"Come here and let me wash that stupid wolfy grin right off your face, you jerkwad." She yanked the hose and while he could have easily held it firmly under his paw, it somehow slipped away, and she sprayed him directly in the nose.

Mik coughed and gagged as the water went down airways it shouldn't. The witch laughed. Like doubled over, funniest thing on the planet laughed. "Ha, ha, ha. Now that's a much better look on you. Offended surprise suits you perfectly."

He lunged at her, and her cry pierced the night. Wait, no. She wasn't screaming in fear of him, she was squealing, and giggling, and running across the yard holding the hose pointed behind her as if the water would keep him at bay.

She wanted a chase? He'd give her a chase. And his tail could shut up about it.

He ran through the grass, dodging her entirely too accurate aim with that damn nozzle. Every time he would be close enough to tackle her to the ground, she would dodge him, and parry that water like a well-timed shot of a gun that shot cold water in his face.

It wasn't the fucking water that stopped him in his tracks each time. No. It was her fucking gleeful giggles at evading him.

Soon enough they were both soaked, and the thin fabric of her nightgown clung to her body in all the right places. Her plump ass alone could drive him to distraction, but her thick thighs, softly rounded belly, and ample breasts were all in second place for his attention.

When he caught her, he was going to enjoy fucking her and spreading his seed all over every curve of her body. He'd wipe away the scent of whatever wolf had previously marked her, and everyone would know that she was his. That is, if she'd use her magic to turn him human again.

"Giving up, puppy? Had enough water up the nose? Gonna be a good pooch now?"

Oh, it was on. Mik crouched low, letting all of his power build up in his legs. She was going down this time, giggles, squeals, water, and all. A moment before he let loose, the witch's hand dropped her side, her body went rigid, and so did his.

Fuck. She was about to have a vision. This was the moment he'd been waiting for. Her eyes went white, and she stared directly at him. Only this time, he didn't see what she saw. A voice not her own came out of her mouth. "Kur was right. You are a douchepotato."

What?

"Listen, I'm not allowed to interfere, but nobody said you couldn't."

"Who are you?" Was his witch possessed by a demon?

"Don't be a dumbass. Who do you think saved your ass from those demons? It's time to repay your debt. Take your mate and get to the Czech countryside near Prague. An old friend of mine is there, and he owes me a favor. You're going to call it in for me."

Mik slowly circled the witch, looking for any telltale signs of shadow. *"Leave this witch be. I owe you no debt, specter, and I have no mate."*

"Don't you though? Who is this then, your dog sitter?" The witch's arm lifted, as if controlled by a puppet master and pointed to herself.

"I said leave her be." He growled, frustrated that he could do nothing. Whoever or whatever this entity was that had taken over her body wasn't going to get hurt if he attacked. Only his witch.

"Oh, you mean like this?" His witch threw her arms up in the air making shapes, danced from side to side, and her voice returned, but singing about staying at random letters of the alphabet. "Y-M-C—"

"Enough. I will not have you humiliating her."

Her arms dropped to her side and she stilled. "She's fine. In her mind she's having a nice cup of tea with a little sumpin sumpin in it. When she wakes up, she'll be nice and relaxed and know nothing of our conversation."

"I want more than a debt repaid if I'm to do your bidding. I'm no one's pawn."

"Ha. Excuse me while I snort-laugh Mikhail Nikolae-vich Volkov. How is your friend Rasputin these days?

37

Hmm? Have you seen much of the rest of the council? Oh, that's right, you haven't since they *murdered* you. But no, no, you were no one's pawn." The way she emphasized the word murder made his ears flatten against his head.

There was no reasoning with this demon or whatever, so he ignored the jabs. "*Either break my curse or tell me how to get this witch to do it, and I will do as you ask and help your friend.*"

Not that he had any idea how he was going to get to Prague. He'd been living as an animal and his life before was completely gone. He didn't exactly have a whole lot of money or resources.

"Break your curse. Yeah, sure. No problem. After you complete the tasks I ask of you."

Tasks, as in many. He was being railroaded. "*Break my curse and give me back my witch. She isn't yours to control.*"

"Oh, she's always been a little bit mine. Your claim on her just seals the deal."

He hadn't claimed her, but he was done arguing. "*You'll leave her to me then?*"

"I'm going to leave you to her, yes. No off you two go, find my friend the black demon dragon, he's a bit lost, and I have important business for him to attend to. Oh, and tell your girl, Kiara here, that the Goddess says hiyee. Sorry I wasn't around to protect her better from those awful one-bloods."

Goddess. Of course. "*Which Goddess are you?*"

Ereshkigal was the most likely candidate since she had

the powers of Hell at her fingertips, and had a whole horde of demon dragons at her disposal. But this entity didn't sound like any ancient Goddess of Death.

The moon above them shined a beam down onto the two of them so bright, it could have been the sun. It swirled around his witch and when it withdrew, her body went limp. Mik bolted forward to give her a softer place to land, among his fur.

She collapsed onto him, and once again, the moment her hands touched him, he shifted into his human form. His curse was once again held at bay.

He wrapped his arms around her and stroked her hair until her eyes fluttered open. She looked up at him and got that same crinkle in her brow as before that displayed how her brain was working hard to process what just happened. "Are you okay, Kiara?"

"I just had the strangest dream about having tea with a rainbow-colored dragon and a Goddess." Her voice came out soft and sleepy. She was so relaxed, she didn't even realize yet that he'd shifted again, and she was in his arms, wet, against his naked chest.

Ah, not Ereshkigal then. If she'd dreamed of that damned dragon, it had to be Inanna. Goddess of Love and War. What a pain in the ass she was going to be.

"She was glowing blue, and looked an awful lot like someone I used to know. Dreams are weird. She said to say hello to you." Her big doe eyes stared up at him as if this was any normal conversation on a sleepy Sunday morning in bed.

"Funny, she told me to say hello to you as well." A shiver rolled through him, and his wolf rose up. Any second now he would shift back again, and lose this calm, easy feeling he had while holding her.

She blinked and tipped her head to the side, exposing the messy mark of another wolf. His fangs elongated and he longed to bite into her soft flesh, make his claim on her as real as the Goddess suggested. She yawned and stretched and then curled deeper into his arms. The urgent need of his wolf to take over again settled.

"You know the Goddess of the Moon?" Her question was so innocent, so naive.

Oh fuck. "I do now."

SWOONTOWN

*S*o, that was weird. Apparently, she'd had some kind of out of body - body snatchers experience where the Goddess of the Moon both served her tea, and spoke to wolf boy through her.

That was a new one.

"We, uh, should probably get inside, and maybe find you some clothes." She shivered, and that was only partially from being soaking wet on a chilly spring night. The way sexy wolf man was looking down at her with those amazing, grey sparkling eyes, he knew the affect he had on her.

This extra ability to touch him and make him shift from wolf to naked porn star was new too. That was fun. Until he looked at her like he wanted to eat her up. Because as much of an asshat as he'd been since the very second he waltzed into her backyard all growly and dominant, she would let him have his way with her.

Like any which way.

That scared the absolute shizz out of her. She didn't want anything to do with wolf mating. Been there, done that, got the scar.

Then why in the world were a whole hurricane of butterflies swirling around in her stomach, and her girly parts, both boobs and her pussy, aching for him to touch her? Maybe because no one had touched her in any way, shape, or form since the night the sheriff marked her.

She was a grown ass, adult woman with needs, and while her battery operated boyfriend did the job most of the time, there was nothing like having a sexy lover, fingers deep inside, telling her to come for him. This guy? Yeah, he wouldn't simply tell her to come, he'd demand it.

And now her mind was all the way in the gutter and there was no rescuing it from the dirty thoughts drain.

"Yes to the going inside." Instead of getting to his feet and helping her up, he just stood, lifting her in a princess style hold, and walked to her back porch door. "The clothing depends on how long you intend to allow your spell over me to last this time."

No man or wolf had ever picked her up and carried her. She wasn't the carrying kind. Too round, too ungainly, too heavy. Even as a kid, her parents had quit picking her up by the time she was in kindergarten. She was woman enough to admit, she was absolutely frickin swooning right now. She certainly wasn't going to say anything about his incorrect presumption that she'd bespelled him until well after he put her down.

He stuck his bare toes into the space between the door and the frame where the screen never completely closed, and yanked it open, then pushed his way inside. His shoulders barely fit through the frame, and he tucked her head against his chest, keeping her safe.

Swoony, swoon, swoontown. She sighed and reveled in the heat of his body. Once in her living room, he released her legs and slowly slid her down his body, chest to chest. The hem of her nightgown caught between them and the farther he lowered her, the higher it rose, until the material pooled around her hips and thighs.

When her feet finally touched the floor and his hard cock pressed against her belly, he grinned down at her, his wolf's fangs still showing, and pushed her up against the back of the door. In a harsh, gutteral tone, he said, "Tell me everything the Goddess showed you."

Without waiting for her to answer, not like she could get her oh, so very dry mouth to work anyway, he pushed his face into the crook of her neck where the scarred mark was. "And where the fucker that marked you is, so I can rip his throat out and claim you myself."

"I don't want anyone to claim me." Liar, lair, wet nightgown on fire. "I told you already, I belong to no one but myself. You can take your patriarchal, misogynistic wolf pack ways and shove them up your ass."

Key grabbed said ass, and somehow accidentally pulled him closer to her, bringing his hips closer to hers. Then her foot, without her consent, lifted up, and she wrapped her leg around the back of his calf.

Dammit, her mind and body were in one hell of a fight at the moment, and it was all ridiculously complicated. Did she want to roll around naked with this man? Yes, very much so, and for a long time, hopefully to include many orgasms.

Had she been around enough wolf society to recognize that this was some kind of pre-mating heat happening between the two of them? Also yes. Poppy and Harley had done it like bunnies on Viagra before their mating. So had Helena and Aleksei. Actually, now that she thought about it, Gal, who'd been mated the longest still showed up pretty much every damn day with a well-loved, satisfied smile on her face.

Wolf shifters were a horny bunch, and their women got the benefit of that.

Key wouldn't say no to those kinds of bennies. She just wanted nothing to do with being claimed, or mated, and especially not marked. That meant she needed to put a full stop to any kind of sexy times with wolf boy. "Galyna Troika murdered him with her teeth to punish him for hurting me and a bunch of other humans. She's very protective of me, and she'd probably do the same to you."

He stilled. "Your mate hurt you?"

God. She didn't want to relive all of this. It had taken her months to claw her way out of the darkness that night had left on her. The warm, if confused, butterflies in her stomach dropped like dead dumb flies and formed a dense ball, heavy with despair, in the pit of her guts. "He was never my mate."

A growl rumbled out of him that was so dark and filled with rage that she should be scared. She wasn't. She reveled in the sound, because it was how she felt on a daily basis. She just never let anyone else see it. Most days she pushed the feelings so deep that she convinced herself she was fine.

She was fine.

Fine.

Key pushed the rage back down where it belonged. Out of mind, out of sight of anyone who might see it.

"Explain," he snarled out his demand.

"No. No, thank you. I'm done now." She moved her hands, sadly, from his butt to his chest and gave him a shove. He didn't move even a centimeter.

"Tell me what happened." His words were clipped, forced, as if he had a hard time getting them to come out of his mouth. He stared down at her, and his eyes didn't just flash with his wolf so close to the surface, they transformed. His wolf was right there, waiting to come out and this time, it wouldn't be wagging its tail. The wolf she saw in him was a beast, and it wanted violence.

Same wolf. Same. But not today. Maybe not ever. She was determined to leave all that behind her. She was healing, god dammit. "Go put some clothes on and we can talk about what happened with the Goddess. That's it. That's all I'm willing to tell you right now."

He didn't do as she said. Of course he didn't. He

pushed up against her, his muscles sinking into her soft body. "You will tell me everything so that when I am tearing everyone he ever knew limb from limb, I can remind them of why they face my wrath. No one but your true mate will ever touch you again."

"You need to work on your anger management skills."

"You need to work on getting angrier."

What? Literally no one had ever said that to her. That wasn't the way to heal trauma. Absolutely not. "I'm about to get angry with you if you don't back off and put some clothes on already."

"I'd like to see you mad." He bared his fangs at her and pushed his nose into her hair. "That would be sexy as fuck."

She rolled her eyes and shoved him again. He still didn't move. "You're confusing passion and rage."

He licked his lip and shifted his focus to her eyes. "Yes, I am."

Oop. Those butterflies just woke back up. "Uh, didn't you want me to tell you about the Goddess?"

"I can scent your arousal, my soft, sweet witch." He took a long, shuddered inhale of breath and made a noise as if he'd smelled the yummiest of fresh pie straight out of the oven. "Changing the subject won't hide the way your body craves what I want to do to you."

Stupid shifters and their extra perceptive senses. "That's only because you're built like a porn star, and I haven't had sex in way too long. So don't read too much into my scent, buster. Nothing a little alone time with my vibrator can't take care of."

His hands went from her sides to grabbing her arms and pinning her wrists against the wall on either side of her head. "No."

Gulp. Was there such a thing as butterfly deterrent? Because she was going to need some. "No, what?"

"You will not be giving yourself any orgasms. I know very well how to use a vibrator to make you come." A strange look crossed his face, as if he'd surprised himself with his own words. His eyes flitted back and forth, accessing thoughts or memories. Then he grinned like the hungry wolf that he was. "In fact, that used to be a particular pastime of mine. That and other instruments of tortuous delights."

She now had the distinct impression she was going to need a safeword. "Look. I don't know you, and you're not getting anywhere near my lady bits with or without a sex toy. I don't even know your name for goodness sake."

"Mikhail."

"Mikhail? Of course it is. Because you couldn't have a boring name like Bob or Sheldon. Regardless if you've got a hot name, a hot body, and a hot temper, we just met, weird shit happened, and we are not having sex."

Mikhail released her hands and pulled away just enough that their bodies weren't mashed together anymore. "Say it again."

"We are not having sex."

"No. My name. Say it again."

"Did I pronounce it wrong? I'm not good at accents, sorry about that." She said his name slower this time, trying her best to be respectful and get it right. "Mikhail."

Before the last syllable was out of her mouth, he'd picked her up by the waist, forcing her to wrap her legs around his hips, and crushed his mouth down on hers. He pushed his tongue in between her lips and stole her breath away. He wanted to take, and she wanted to give.

Key shoved her hands into his hair and held his lips tight to hers, kissing and tasting, and dueling against his need with her own. The scrape of his beard across the skin of her cheek and chin as he turned his head for another angle, shot tingles from her throat to her core. She moaned and ground her pelvis against him.

He broke the kiss and lowered his mouth to her throat and hissed against her skin.

As quickly as he'd grabbed her up and kissed her, he set her down and took a giant step away. Key swayed and set her hands against the wall to steady herself. Mikhail's chest heaved with his harsh breathing. "I will fuck you, Kiara. You will cry out my name as I make you come again and again. After we do the Goddess's bidding."

What the actual fucktarts? "You are one confusing asshat."

But she was grateful for the reprieve. There was something much more going on between them than lust, and if she was going to get naked and have some fun times with any man, supernatural or not, she wanted to be in control of herself and her emotions.

Mikhail had her mind and body doing gymnastics and this tumultuousness was going to break down all her carefully built barriers that held her together every day. "Yeah. Fine. This is fine. I'm going to get you some sweatpants that I think are the only thing I have that will maybe fit you, and then we will sit on opposite sides of my living room so you can tell me what the Goddess's bidding is. Okay?"

"You don't know?"

"I never know what comes out of my mouth when I go all psychic visiony. So unless you remember, I'm not going to be any help."

Mikhail frowned at her, got that look everyone did when she told them about the giant disconnect in her special power. People usually thought she was lying, but to what end? She didn't like looking stupid any more than they did.

Whatever. She turned her back on him, yanked her still wet nightgown down so he wasn't watching her bare ass jiggle as she walked away, and headed down the hallway to her bedroom. She grabbed her last clean nightgown, unfortunately a shorter and thinner one, and changed quickly. Then she dug around for those sweats she had but never wore.

"I'm not sure why you offered to clothe me when you weren't going to allow me to stay in human form." His voice popped into her head just as she found the grey sweatpants in question.

Key hurried back out to the living room to find

Mikhail's huge wolf smooshing one corner of her couch. He growled at her, and she threw the pants at his face. He caught them and flung them around like a chew toy. "I'm not sure why you keep thinking I have anything to do with you shifting. I already told you, I'm not a witch, I don't know any spells, and I certainly don't know how to break a curse."

Mikhail barked at her and then whined, laid down on the couch, breaking the legs of it under his weight, and gave her the saddest puppy dog eyes she'd ever seen. "Don't you try to manipulate me with that ASPCA commercial look."

He huffed and got up, taking the whole three enormous wolf steps toward her, and stuck his nose directly in between her legs like someone's ill trained pet. Poof. Just like that, he was on his knees in front of her with his very human head and mouth and teeth between her thighs, licking at her sensitive skin.

Huh. That was the third time she'd touched him, and he'd spontaneously shifted. Maybe she did have some magic power to make him human. It didn't seem to last very long if she wasn't actively touching him though. If they had to do some kind of mission for the Goddess together, that was going to get awkwardly uncomfortable to be all up in each other's space all the time.

She was about to say so, but forgot how to talk when he pressed a kiss to her pussy. A french kiss.

DUNGEONS AND DRAGONS

$\mathcal{M}$ ik had surprised himself with the memories of spending his time at any number of the Volkov's sex clubs dotted across Europe. All he could think about right now was fucking Kiara, and the thought of any other women, especially those of his past life made his teeth hurt.

He'd used the dungeons and willing submissives to blow off steam and work out his frustrations of trying to lead a people long in the dark into a new and better world. He'd dragged Niko to quite a few when his friend had served him in the Wolf Tzar's guard.

Never once, in any of his filthy debauched evenings had he ever licked a pussy. His Volkov mentors made sure he knew that women were made to serve him and give him pleasure. Not the other way around.

Sure, he knew the finer points of making a woman come, but on his terms, and usually after a long bout of denial, spankings, and taking his own satisfaction in her body first. He'd even turned up his nose at men who went down on their partners.

This was just one more lesson from his past life he had to unlearn. Because if those schmoes knew the unadulterated thrill in hearing a woman moan when he licked her clit, or the way she tasted of sweet and salty, spiced ripe peaches, they'd all have their heads between their ladies legs exactly like he did right now.

"Oh good gravy, Mikhail. You should probably stop. Oh, oh, right there." She slid her fingers into his hair just like she had when he kissed her before and guided his mouth the spot she needed him most.

Kiara wasn't wrong when she'd said he had sex and violence mixed up in his head. There was a very fine line between the two when he craved both so fervently. The violence in his beast won his mind hands down. The longer he remained in his wolf form the deeper and darker his need to hurt, torture, and kill grew.

Except with her.

She moaned again and Mik paid very close attention to what he was doing that made her respond with those breathy sounds. His own cock ached and pulsed between his legs, and somehow that made everything he did for her even better.

Kiara gripped his hair tight, sending tingles through his scalp and then all of a sudden, her hand went slack, and her moans went silent. Mik's chest constricted as did hers when she was about to have a vision. Fucking piss poor timing, Goddess.

Dammit. If he knew how, he'd make the Goddess pay for this.

Mik carefully supported her body and stood up in front of her, holding her in his arms. He waited for either the vision to hit him too, or the Goddess to communicate through her again.

Her eyes went white, and he got the images of a rainbow, golden wings, a wedding reception, a bright green flash of light, and a stack of hay. What the fuck was any of that supposed to mean? Not helpful.

Kiara's mouth opened and this time, in her own voice, not the Goddess's, she said, "Welcome to DragonAir. We know you have no choice when flying, so we appreciate your business. Please board and find your seat promptly for our transatlantic flight leaving this evening. The temperature will be a balmy zero degrees, so do dress warmly. Beverage service will not be available, and we suggest you pack accordingly."

What the fuck?

Kiara blinked and sucked in a deep breath. Her eyes cleared and she stared up at him with an expression that mirrored how he felt. "Weren't you doing something very different a moment ago? Ah, shit. I had a vision, didn't I?"

Her shoulders sunk and she made a tsk sound of irritation. "Now this damn wretched ability is screwing around with my sex life too? I'm pretty sure I was moments away from some freaky deaky fireworks thanks to your very talented tongue, and now, nothing. Not even a tingle down there. Grr."

He squeezed her tighter and tugged a coil of her hair. "Was that your growl? We really do need to work on your violent tendencies."

She narrowed her eyes at him, and then pasted on a big, fake-ass smile. "It's fine. I'm fine. That's the most action I've gotten in a long time, and I'm grateful for it. Now, tell me what I said and—"

Nope. She wasn't getting away with this. Not on his watch. "What are you doing? You're grateful?"

"Yep. Very, very grateful. Did you know that when you're unhappy, practicing gratitude can actually change your brain chemistry? I learned that in therapy." Her smile didn't waver even a little bit, in fact, it grew, but it never reached her eyes.

"Hmm." He gave her his most stern eyebrow raise. "I'd rather rip someone's throat out."

She nodded like she was considering what he was saying. She wasn't. "You know what else I'm grateful for? Apple pie moonshine."

Kiara slipped out of his arms, still babbling, but took his hand in hers and led him to her kitchen. "Have you had it? Probably not. You're a vodka guy, am I right? It's pretty similar. You'll see."

She let go to reach for a cupboard door but gasped and grabbed his hand again. "I think your shifty-ness is connected to touching me. So how about you hang onto me while I make our drinks."

He'd come to the same conclusion. Perhaps it wasn't her magic that pushed his curse away, but if not that, then what?

With a deft spin, she turned back to her kitchen counter, while wrapping his arm around her waist. He didn't need a drink, and he certainly didn't like how she pushed her emotions down. She was running from them like a scared little mouse, when she was truly a proud, powerful, and passionate woman who should be scared of nothing. He would fight every battle going on inside her head for her if he had to. "Kiara. The sun is about to come up, and we appear to have a flight to catch with a dragon."

She shook her head and reached for a glass. "Dragons again, huh? I am so grateful for dragons in my life."

He took the glass from her and crushed it in his hand. Shards sliced his hand open, and the blood dripped through his fist. His wolf's healing ability surged up and closed the wounds almost as fast as he'd made them. "I don't think gratitude means what you think it means."

Kiara silently opened his hand, and carefully picked out the glass, dropping it into the nearby sink. She wet a paper towel and dabbed at the red, angry lines where the cuts had been, wiping away the blood. In a quiet voice, that didn't waver like it had before, she said, "Never go against a psychic when death is on the line, Dread Pirate Westley."

He didn't know what she meant, but the strength in her voice was better. His witch was back again. "Mik."

"What?" She turned in his arms to face him.

"Call me Mik. It's what my friends, or the friends I used to have, called me." He had no friends anymore, and he didn't fucking need them.

"Dread Pirate Mik, it is." A genuine smile lifted her lips this time.

"Unless I'm making you come. If want to practice your gratitude, you can thank me for your orgasms by screaming my name."

"You haven't even made me come yet, so cool your jets there, you-can-thank-me Mik."

If this was his old life, he'd take her over his knee, spank her, and call her a brat. Then he'd make her apologize on her knees. With his cock down her throat. "Is that a challenge?"

"Yes. But for later when there are fewer dragons and goddesses in our way."

Ah, yes. The mission from the Goddess, and the impending flight with the dragon. Fucking would have to wait. He wasn't used to waiting for anything. "Your vision suggested you dress warmly. I believe we are being provided with a ride to the Czech countryside via dragon."

"Umm, excuse me what now?" She pulled away, but he did not let her go. "I can't go to the Czech Republic? I have to work. I have bills to pay."

"The Goddess has demanded we do her bidding. Then she's promised to lift my curse." She hadn't exactly specified that Kiara had to go with him, but he was not letting her out of his sight, or reach.

"What do you mean she can lift your curse?" She sucked her lower lip between her teeth and worked it while her brain processed her own question. "Can she lift mine?"

Could she? Yes. Would she? That was another matter. Especially since her visions were a gift from the Goddess in the first place. It may have been forced upon her, but it was a gift nonetheless. "She is a Goddess. The Universe is at her whim."

"Well, then let's go get dressed." She tugged him out of the kitchen and to her bedroom. There was already an array of clothes strewn about, but she pulled opened drawers and closet doors with her free hand and threw more clothes onto her bed. "Are we talking winter boots, ski pants, and parkas, or are jeans and a sweater good?"

"Wear what you will be most comfortable in. I will keep you warm." And safe.

That thought filtered its way into his mind unbidden. She was his to command, to pleasure if he wished, but most importantly, to use to help him break free from the curses Hell had wrought upon him. Only then could he retake his rightful place in the world and wreak his vengeance. He'd do well to remember that.

She was a tool. Not his mate.

When he was in his wolf form, he hadn't questioned that goal. As a man, he could think more easily, but it seemed he could also be swayed by the temptation of sex and satisfaction. Being back in this form had given him a rush of emotions that his beast had been able to hold at bay.

He craved the control he was so famous for in his former life, not to be ruled by man's emotions or beast's instincts. That was the end game here. Not her.

"Is that an innuendo or can you really keep me warm? Can you shift into your wolf form when we're touching? We should experiment with that."

The way she'd gone from sullen and stroppy to filled with excitement and life gave him the feeling this sunshiny version of her was the one filled with the passion that drew his wolf to her in the first place. This was the real her, and whatever trauma she'd suffered at the hands of the wolf who'd marked her had eaten away at her soul.

He could relate.

"I have no idea if I can shift when you touch me." This was the first time he'd been anything but the wolf since his return from Hell. We will practice until we find the dragon. I will see if I can shift while you touch me, and you will learn to harness your visions."

He'd seen other women gain powers like hers when they were marked and mated. The Volkovs had been experimenting with exactly this phenomenon before his death. Something a very small inner circle knew about. Only a small percentage of those who'd developed psychic gifts had been able to control them, and no one had yet figured out the common denominator between them.

But he also knew that both Niko and Kosta's mates had developed these abilities, and they used them to help their mates rule over their packs.

"You don't know what you're talking about. If I could control it, don't you think I would have already learned how?" Gone was the excitement, replaced by her ire." I've had three already today, if you don't count the whole body snatchers thing. Which had been an unusual shit-show. You think I want to go around spewing weird prophecies? No. It's ruined my life, and if this Goddess of yours can take it away, then dammit, she's going to."

The white fog of a vision passed over her eyes but rolled though and was gone. She clenched her fists, squeezing his hand so tight, if he weren't a wolf, she might have broken the bones.

"I have no power over my visions. They control me, not the other way around."

That didn't appear to be entirely true.

If he trusted Niko at all, he would be taking her to his old friend and asking his mate to help Kiara. No, it was better to do this on their own. They would both earn the Goddess's favor and make her fix everything.

Mik pulled her from her rank and task of finding clothes and into his arms. She wiggled against him, angry and bratty. He gripped the hair at the back of her scalp, pulled it tight into his fist, and tilted her head back so she was forced to look up at him.

"Shh, witch. Stop your complaining. Either you can get mad and harness that energy, or you can fight against the fate you think you've been given. But you cannot simply smile and give in."

"You're hurting me."

Not physically, he wasn't. He tugged her hair a bit harder to show her so. "I know. Now, I can whisper filthy sweet nothings into your ear and comfort you, or I can take you over my knee and spank your plump ass for being a brat. I don't usually let anyone choose, but I will you, just to see what you decide."

Her cheeks and throat flushed at his words and her pupils went blown and dark. She didn't want to like the idea of being spanked, but she did. When they had more time, he would teach her to enjoy some pain with her pleasure.

"I don't need comforting, and I certainly don't want you to... spank me." She glanced away and squirmed in his arms. "I'll remember not to let you see my frustration about my so-called gift if it makes you all riled up like this. So, you can let go now, and let me get dressed."

"I told you, Kiara, you are mine. You will not and can not hide anything from me. That includes your emotions."

She narrowed her eyes at him. "Watch me, buster. Now put on some damn pants."

KETCHER FAST

*O*kay, first of all, Key didn't know dragons came in rainbow colors, and second of all, when she'd found out they were going on some super-secret sneaky mission for the Goddess of the Moon, she didn't expect to end up dancing with Mik at the Ketcher-Fast wedding reception.

"Did it not seem strange to you that we just happened to catch that groomsmen and bridesmaid tossing their clothes off right when we needed them, and that they both just happened to wear our sizes?" The pretty pink plus-size dress Key had literally stolen from some poor, unsuspecting, but seemingly very happy and preoccupied, woman fit her perfectly. She didn't even need any dreaded shapewear.

Boy, oh boy, did Mik fill out a tux. She thought they'd skulk around trying not to be seen, but Mik had dragged her right out onto the dance floor and had half the women in the room swooning over the way he shook his groove thang. He dipped her just like you'd see in the movies, and it had her breathless. "The Goddess works in mysterious ways."

The music slowed, and she was ready to pull away and go sit at a table and steal somebody's slice of cake. He pulled her closer, wrapping one arm around her waist and swayed his hips in time to the music. She couldn't help but match his rhythm. "But why are we here? I thought you said we were going to Prague."

"I don't know, but I smell both demons and a green dragon warrior all over this building, so there must be something she wants us to see or do here first. Keep your eye out for any demons." He led her through slow, easy steps, turning them slowly so they both got a view of the whole room.

"Uh, I do not know, nor do I want to know, what demons look like. That's what you're for." The Troikas had reported fighting demons before, but as they always did, they kept her sheltered from any of that. As soon as Gal or Poppy discovered she was missing, they were going to freak out. She should have left them a note or something.

"I will not let anyone touch you, much less a demon." His words were loud enough that the nearest couple gave them a look and moved away. That didn't even faze Mik. Which did something warm to her insides. Whew. Was it getting warmer in here?

He lowered his hand from the small of her back to her

butt and drew her body closer to his. "You may not recognize the dragon as he will likely also be hiding in human form. But demons cannot shift, they smell of Hell, and will come out of the Shadow. You can't miss them. They look a lot like a bat and an ostrich had an evil chaos baby and it's cranky."

Right. She would definitely notice that. Just like the way she noticed the way his hard on pressed against her belly. Again. Was this man ever not hard?

A lot of the guests were filtering out, and Key saw the bride wave over a really pretty woman with a clipboard and a headset, who must be the wedding planner. Looked as though they were ushering drunk guests out one particular door. Must be to rooms, or maybe limos. How very organized. So, definitely not demons then.

He spun her around, never once letting go of her hand, then pulled her right back into his very deft arms. Lord love a man who knew how to dance well.

A stunning older woman, weirdly dressed all in white, who was on the floor with her husband, who wore a very bright rainbow tie and pocket hanky, winked at her as they danced by. "You know what they say about a man who can dance well. You're a very lucky lady."

If Mik's promises to do lots of filthy things to her, and the small taste of said things were any indication, that woman was right. It did seem strange to her that she was so drawn to him, and completely unbothered by the fact that they'd gotten pretty damn intimate moments after they'd met. She shouldn't be attracted to him, much less feel so comfortable both in his arms and in his company.

But she did.

Unlike the Troikas, who tried to make her feel safe, Mik actually did. Just by holding her close and making promises about the death of people or demons who touched her.

The band finished their song and did not immediately start a new one. They appeared to be packing up their instruments. That was too bad, she could have danced all night, and still have begged for more. How had she not noticed they were the last ones on the dance floor? "I think our cover is going to be blown in a minute. The wedding reception seems to be over, and I didn't even get any cake."

"The dragon is close. Come on." Mik pulled her over to a table and shoved her underneath of it. What the hell? He let go of her hand and shit, he was going to shift. It would be bad if he attacked a dragon before everyone had left the reception. She reached out to at least grab a hold of his leg before that could happen, and she got a piece of cake on a plate shoved into it.

Mik followed, crawling in after her. She opened her mouth to chastise him, and he shoved a bite of cake into her mouth. "Shh. The dragon warrior is here."

A woman's legs, sans shoes, appeared under the table-cloth as she sat down, and a fork clinked against a plate from above. She blew out a long, tired breath, and Key held hers.

"Stop right there, thief." The deep rumble of a male voice sounded, and Mik held his fingers to his lips, but mouthed 'dragon.'

The legs pushed the chair back and stood up. "I'm just doing a bit of quality control. Have to make sure the cake is up to Willingham Weddings standards."

Ha. That was a good excuse for the wedding planner to snag a piece of cake... after the reception was over.

He growled at her. Oh, yeah. That was definitely some kind of shifter dude. They were all very growly like that. "I don't give a damn about the cake, unless that is where you've hidden my goods."

"Your goods?" Uh-oh. Wedding lady was pissed now.

"First of all, you have to tell me what brand of toothpaste you use, and second, back up out of my business, buster."

Ooh. She was about to tell him what for. This was going to be good. Key took another bite of cake and waggled her eyebrows at Mik. He wasn't enjoying this nearly as much as she was.

"Do not try to beguile me with your talk of hygiene products, your hair of gold, and your body made for sin. Where have you hidden my Wyr relic, witch?"

"Stop staring at my tuchis. Whatever you're looking for ain't in there."

"Stop enticing me with your curves, thief. You cannot distract me from what is mine."

Wedding planner coughed all offended like and Key sure wished she could get a view of what was going down. She inched toward the edge of the table, but Mik grabbed her and pulled her into his lap. Okay. This was nice too. She didn't even protest when he slid his hand over her mouth.

That part was kind of hot. Oh geez. There was Mik's cock poking into her backside.

"Are you ill?" Dragon dude did not get what was going on. "I won't have you dying before you tell me where the statue is hidden."

What an asshat. Must run in the shifter blood.

"I think maybe we've gotten off on the wrong foot here. I'm Ciara Mosley-Willingham." She paused for a full count of ten, where clearly dragon dude was supposed to say his name. "And you are?"

"Wondering what kind of spell you're trying to work on me. Whatever it is, I assure you a Wyvern is immune."

What was a why Vern? She was going to need a dragon dictionary if she was going to be hanging around these guys for the Goddess. Hopefully Mik knew some of this jargon.

"I was trying to be nice, but I've had a very long and tiring day, so my patience is wearing thin. I don't have your thingy, and I don't know what a why Vern is. I thought for a minute I might help you try to find it, but I'm done now." She walked away but didn't get very far.

"As am I. If you won't return what you have taken from me, I will be forced to bring you before the AllWyr council."

Add 'all weird' to the dragon stuff dictionary.

"What the hell?" The bare feet Key had been watching suddenly went skittering across the floor as if she was being dragged away. Key bit Mik's finger and he removed his hand. She twisted and pressed her lips to his ear so she could whisper as quietly as possible. "We have to do something. What if he hurts her?"

"Hey, stop right this instant or I'll bring out the self-defense moves."

Mik shook his head. "The witch can take care of herself just fine. Besides, this isn't the one we're meant to help, so keep quiet and pay attention. The Goddess wants us to learn something for our task."

"Save your defense for the council. You'll need it," the dragon threatened but his voice was much further away.

Where was he taking her. Key didn't like this one bit and she would not stand by while a woman was being kidnapped by a shifter. Her vision went all fuzzy and black. Not like a vision. No this was her own system pumping her up with adrenaline for a fight.

She yanked at the arms holding her and scrambled on her hands and knees out from under the table. Oh God, she was right. The dragon man was forcibly dragging her away. Key hurried through the gaunlet of tables and chairs, grabbing two forks to use as weapons along the way.

It was hard to see where she was going and what she was grabbing in this intense green light that filled the entire room.

"Let me go," the woman cried.

A grey blur whooshed past Key and in an instant her wolf blocked her way. *"Kiara, don't interfere. The dragon will not hurt that witch. Can you not see how his soul shard is alight for her? She is his mate."*

Mik moved aside just enough so that she could see their interaction, but moved each time she did, not letting her get any closer.

"Return my relic."

"I'm gonna make you a relic."

"Save your spells, witch."

"Your face is a witch."

The scary dragon released the woman and grabbed at his face. When he didn't find anything wrong with it, he narrowed his eyes and glared at her. "Good try, witch. You'll pay for that."

Oh no. No, no, no. He was going to hurt her, bite her, make her into his slave. Sometimes horrible men who thought they were your mate hurt unsuspecting women. Key tried to run toward them, but she ran right into a giant wall of fur, which changed quickly into a mostly naked man wearing only tatters of a perfectly ruined tux.

He tucked her face into his shoulder and stroked her hair. He clasped her even tighter when the woman squealed, and the sound faded as it got farther away. "Shh, shh, shh. It's okay, *pchelka*."

She didn't want him to see her tears, so instead she glanced up, and saw, flying above the city, the giant wings, flapping gracefully through the sky, of an enormous green dragon, with a flopping and flailing woman clasped in its talons.

"Well," the older man with the rainbow tie sidled up to them and stared out into the night at the retreating form of the dragon. "That was fun. Shall we follow them to Czechia? Once she's there, Jett will come out of hiding and you can set him on the right path, eh? Lots to do. Places to see, people to do. Let's go, kids."

In a flash of light that practically blinded her, the man turned into the very same rainbow dragon with the wonky wing that had flown them from Rogue to this wedding reception. He grabbed them both and caged them into his talons and jumped right off the same balcony the green dragon had dragged the wedding planner.

He flew them gracefully up much higher into the sky than the green dragon, and beyond a group of gold dragons riding on some air currents. None of them seemed to notice the rainbow dragon or the two of them at all.

The air up here was indeed cold and Key huddled close to Mik. "I'm mad at you, so don't think you can do any funny business with your naked parts right now, mister wolf."

"You can take all your anger out on me when we aren't a thousand feet over the ocean. I will relish every second of you letting your ire out where it should be. But it's not really me your angry with, is it?"

No. It wasn't. "Shush your face, and don't you dare say

I'm cute when I'm mad, or I will shove your right off this dragon, and you can swim to Europe."

"Ah, but who will keep you warm if you do?" He pressed his mouth to her temple and huffed out a long, labored breath. Fur sprouted from his arms and chest, wrapping her up as if he was a big fluffy wolf blanket.

Huh. Guess he'd made progress on trying to shift when she was touching him. She sure as shinola wished she'd learned even a modicum of control over her visions. Maybe she could have seen what the holy hell was going to happen tonight and avoided the whole shit show. Except that cake. That was really good cake.

She sulked for a little while longer in the cold air and silence. Mik didn't pressure her to say anything more, but she could practically feel him seething under all that fur. "I don't like feeling used."

"No, you wouldn't. I don't like it much either. Let that fuel us when we get to our destination so we can complete this task and be done with the whole lot of them, dragons and Goddesses."

Fine by her. If she never saw another dragon, goddess, or wolf ever again, that would be too soon. Except Mik. She would keep him.

DEMONS & DRAGONS & UNICORNS, OH MY

*T*hat fucking dragon dropped them off in the middle of a forest near some train tracks without so much as a suggestion of what they were looking for. Mik was fine in the wilderness on his own, but Kiara was not. She was cold, she was hungry, and she wouldn't complain about either to save her life.

She was fine, she said.

He was beginning to hate the word fine.

In fact, he might murder her the next time she told him she was fine. No, he wouldn't wish the demons of hell on anyone but those who betrayed him. He was going to make good on that promise to take her over his knees and spank her ass until she either cried or came.

Her fucking emotions were so bottled up he wouldn't be surprised if she did both at the same time. He'd like to be the one to push her over that edge.

No wonder she couldn't harness her own powers. They could really use a vision right about now to tell them what the hell they were supposed to be doing.

Kiara rubbed her hands together over the small fire she'd made out of twigs. "See, I told you I had finely honed Girl Scouting skills. All we need now are some marshmallows and a song book, and we'd have ourselves a good old-fashioned camp out while we wait for the Goddess's dragon friend."

Mik stretched out beside her and rolled around in the dirt to get the scent of dragon off. He still couldn't hold on to his human form for longer than a few seconds after she stopped touching him. The flight across the ocean was the longest he'd been human in a long time.

It had given him too much space to think and remember. His old life had been a shitshow. This mission, the adventure with Kiara, was simple and easy. Yes, they'd been running around in the unknown with little information, but he knew exactly what needed to be done and what the result would be.

Being the Wolf Tzar was... complicated.

"I can think of a better way to spend our time waiting." Not to mention covering himself in her ripe peaches scent instead of the burnt cookie smell of that dragon.

She threw a stick at him. "I may only be wearing this scrap of a dress, but I'm not taking it off."

"No one said you had to take the dress off. I'll take you on your hands and knees, dress pushed up over your head, fucking

you from behind. That would warm you up better than your fire that's about to go out."

The scent of her arousal at his words floated to him and he reveled in it. She may try her best to suppress her other emotions, but her lust would not be bound. Perhaps that was the emotion he should push her tap into that could help her access her power.

"I, uh, I need more firewood." She jumped up and hurried over to the mostly dead tree she'd picked most of the undergrowth branches off already. Her arms mid-air, she froze, and Mik's muscles in his chest clenched.

Fuck. She was having a vision. He leaped to her side and sniffed the air around him, searching for the object of her vision. The images of half a dozen women with charms of green, blue, gold, and red dangling around their necks filtered through his mind. Each one stood oblivious as the hand of a black demon dragon tried to snatch the glowing shards from them. Behind them all stood a small girl, with fire in her eyes and daggers in her hands, who screamed and yelled at the women, as if she was trying to warn them, but they couldn't hear her. Then the scene switched to one of those quaint German towns, with snow gently falling, and a blonde, curvy woman, wearing a t-shirt with a childish design on it, standing at a food cart ordering a drink.

What the hell was this supposed to mean, and who was it for?

"Green and gold are not your colors. The souls you

seek are meant for others, and will not give you what you want. Try the unicorn at the Christmas mart."

Mik growled at the form coming out of the shadows in front of them. This scruffy looking mess of a man was the source of the burnt cookies smell, not their rainbow dragon. He wore next to nothing even though dragon shifters had the ability to shift their clothes and possessions along with them. He didn't look as though he owned a thing in the world.

He was also no ordinary dragon warrior. He reeked of the taint of Hell. This not-dragon stared at Kiara with a feral look in his eye. "What the fuck is that supposed to mean?"

Mik put himself between the intruder and Kiara. She slid a hand into his fur, and he shifted instantly for her. "Don't come any closer, demon. This witch has a message for you, but you touch her, and it will be the last message you ever receive."

Kiara sighed. "I'm not a witch. But I'm guessing I just said something weird. I don't even know what came out of my mouth, much less what it means."

The stinky demon dragon circled them but kept his distance. He eyed the two of them up and down, his gaze locking on to where Kiara's hand gripped Mik's shoulder. "Then why did you say it?"

"I don't have any control over my visions." She rolled her eyes at him, frustrated to have to explain again. Mik liked the flavor of that bitter chocolate scent coming from her. His witch wasn't as soft and compliant as a few days ago, and that was delicious. "You have to figure out what it means."

The demon dragon stopped, sniffed the wind and listened for something. Whatever he waited or searched for wasn't there, so he refocused on the two of them. "Who told you to say it to me?"

Mik didn't like this guy. He didn't like any dragons, but the stench of Hell on him had Mik's teeth on edge. How did the Goddess know this beast, and why would she want him to do her a favor? He wasn't one of her people. That feeling of being used sank low in Mik's stomach. There was much more going on here than any of them were privy to.

He refused to be a fucking pawn to Gods and Goddesses.

Kiara slid her had lower and slipped it into his. He squeezed it tight but didn't move to stand in front of her or pull her into his arms. She was standing her ground and not backing down from the demon dragon's gruff demeanor. He'd allow her to bask in that confidence. It was good for her.

Besides, he would tear this man's head off if he moved even an inch closer, and they both knew it. "Oh, umm, nobody told me to. But the Goddess of the Moon did send us to find you. I mean, I think it's you we were supposed to find. Do you know her?"

The demon dragon growled, and his beast rose up to the surface, flickering through his eyes. With the little control Mik had over his shift, he let his fangs drop and his own wolf flashed in his eyes, warning his adversary of the violence in his soul.

He didn't back off, but his dragon inside went no further with its intended strike. "I have fought by her side. But she has no business interfering in the affairs of dragons."

Kiara held up one palm, placating the demon's foul attitude. His ire alone was enough for Mik to tear out the demon's eyeballs. He would have already if she wasn't here to keep his mind clear and calm. "She knows that. It's why she sent us in her stead. She says you owe her a favor and is calling it in."

"My path is my own, and for my brethren, not her. You can tell the Goddess to fuck off and mind her own people. You're not the first wolf I've seen corrupted by the forces of Hell."

A broken place inside Mik's heart cracked and the darkness he'd kept at bay since he'd first scented Kiara poured out. His claws burst forth, his bones cracked and reformed, his skin split, and he lunged for the demon dragon, fully in beast mode.

No one talked to Kiara like that and lived to do it again.

The demon shifted into a huge black dragon and shot a stream of hellfire at Mik. It missed by a mile, giving a warning instead of injury. Something else caught his attention and he took flight, jumping up above the trees. "*Take your mate and leave this place quickly. A horde of demon wyrms is after the Green Wyvern's mate and you don't want to be in their way when they come trampling through here."*

He flew deftly into the night and Mik heard a crashing of branches not far from them.

Demons. Fuck.

"I sure hope that fulfills the task she asked of us. I have a feeling the Goddess isn't going to like that we didn't convince him to go back with us." Kiara threw her hands up and looked in the direction the dragon had flown in. "Shoot. I bet he was supposed to be our ride back too. What are we going to do now?"

"Run."

"What?" She looked at him like he was on drugs.

She hadn't heard what the dragon said. It must have been an alpha-to-alpha thing. Mik pushed an image into her head of what a horde of demon wyrms stampeding at them would look like.

"Holy piles of crap. That's what a demon looks like. Yes, let's run. Run far, far away from that." She slipped off the silly, but sexy as shit, pink high heels that matched her dress and brandished them like weapons. "Where to?"

"The train tracks through those trees. There's a station about a thousand meters to the west. I can feel the beat of the train not far. Get to that station as fast as you can. Get on that train, no matter what you have to do. Get on it."

"Wait, where are you going to be?"

"I will hold the horde off as long as I can."

"Oh no, no, no." She shook her head and brandished one of her shoe weapons at him. "You are not sacrificing yourself for me and leaving me in the middle of nowhere all alone."

Screeches and crashes exploded far too closely, and they were out of time. Mik growled and snapped at Kiara's heels. *"Run. Now."*

Her eyes went wide and in an instant, she turned and sprinted toward the train tracks. Mik spun on his heel and faced a trio of demon wyrms stalking closer. These were the really dumb but fierce ones. He'd destroyed his fair share of these in Hell.

This was going to be fun. He let the red anger and violence of his wolf completely take over. He forgot all about the Goddess, the demon dragon, and even Kiara, and sunk into the darkness of death and despair once again. But this time it wasn't his death, nor his despair. He was returning those curses to Hell along with these minions of Ereshkigal and her progeny.

The little beasties advanced on him, and it took Mik only moments to tear them apart and spit the black oil of their remains out onto the ground. In the woods ahead of him, trees bent in an unnatural way, forming an archway in the forest. More demon wyrms surrounded and crawled along the barrier, reaching in and grasping for something.

The more of them he could take out now, the less would be in pursuit of his mate.

His. Mate.

Mark.

Claim.

Mate.

Yes, she was his and he would not allow anyone or anything to hurt her ever again. That included the forces of Hell that had tortured him after death. They had no place in this new life. A life he needed to learn to be grateful for.

Mik ran along one side of the arch of trees, the black demon dragon flew along the other. Together they tore demon wyrms down, littering the forest floor with their oily remains. Until the witch inside emerged and almost ran smack into the side of the train waiting on the tracks.

She circled around, looking worse for the wear, and onto the platform. She ducked into the train to safety. But where was Kiara?

Mik put his nose to the ground and searched for her ripe peaches scent. *"Kiara, pchelka, where are you?"*

Dammit. If he'd fucking marked her she would be able to respond to him as a proper mate. But no, he had to be the asshole and pretend her soul didn't light his up like a sunny day. He didn't think he wanted a mate, but he did want her.

The train whistle blew its signal that it was leaving the station, and at the very last second, Kiara came bursting out of the trees. She had a whole bird's nest in her hair, only one shoe, and looked like she could take on the whole world. She wasn't even injured. She ran onto the platform and slipped onto the train a second before the doors closed.

Good. She was safe and would be at least warmer on

the train than in these fates forsaken woods. Mik would run along behind the train as it wound its way to Prague. He needed the time to figure out how to woo Kiara into letting him mark her and claim her.

She wouldn't want his bite and he had no idea what would happen to her gift when he did.

I'M A SNACK

*W*ithout a cell phone with GPS, or at least a compass, Key could get lost in her own closet. The dark woods of the Czech Republic, barefoot, cold, without her wolf, and scared out of her mind, was a friggin' nightmare. Everywhere she looked, she saw red devil eyes.

She heard the screeches of the creatures and could only hope that it was the sound they made when Mik or that dragon guy were killing them.

Okay, okay. But Mik wouldn't have sent her running off on her own if he didn't think she could do this. Best to just keep running. Something glinted in the light up ahead and god, it had better be the train. A whistle blew, and it was as if her heart was singing along with relief. Almost there.

She stumbled forward and her heart jumped straight up into her throat at the squawk of a beast in the trees above her. A demon wyrm jumped down from the branches and hissed at her. She gasped and swore at the same time which just made a weird dying baby animal sound.

"Get away from me, you disgusting lizard." She didn't want to scream, because that might distract Mik from his own killing spree, and a distraction could mean the wrong death.

Key could not take losing another thing that was important to her in this life. Not. One. More. Thing. She shouldn't have left Mik's side. He was lost without her, or maybe she was the one lost without him.

The demon wyrm lunged at her, snapping its teeth and hissing. "You snack."

Uh, rude. "Yeah, I am a snack, and you can eat a bag of dicks."

No more missus nice guy. Key called upon her self-defense moves and popped the wyrm right in the solar plexus, or at least where that would be on a human. Then she stomped on its instep, because that hurt like a mother. It hissed and spit hot dribbles of fire at her and she'd had enough.

"Okay, now I'm mad and I'm all out of gratitude, but I do have this." She shoved her sparkly pink high heel right up its nose and kicked it in the groin with her bare foot. The creature burst into a puff of black smoke and disintegrated into a pile of oily goo, right at her feet. The high heel dissolved in its remains.

Ew. But also... fucking awesome.

Maybe Mik was right, and she should let her anger out a little more often.

"Kiara, pchelka, *where are you?"* Mik's voice burst into her head and she spun, looking for him. But there was nothing around her but trees and trains. She should have asked him how that whole mindspeak thing worked and how to do it back.

But as hard as she thought words in her brain, there was no response. He'd told her to get on that train no matter what, so that's what she was going to do. He'd better be either on it, or waiting for her wherever it dropped her off.

The tree line broke a few feet ahead and she ran toward the train so fast she gave herself a stitch. With her last bit of energy, she ran along the track and up to a Soviet era style, cement train platform. She climbed up the three metal steps and into the train car, just as the doors were closing. The whistle blew again, and the train jerked, lurching forward. It took an interminably long time to move past the platform and away from the black stain of the dead demon she'd left on the forest floor.

She'd done that. She'd killed a demon, and she'd liked it. A Katy Perry tune popped into her head and she couldn't help but sing along. "I killed a wyrm, and I liked ih-it, the taste of power when I whacked it."

Now to find Mik. She pushed the door open and found rows of bench seats, with only a few sleepy riders. The trees were whipping past the windows, but she caught sight of a wolf running alongside. Yes. There was that telltale glow he had.

Key waved frantically, hoping he would see her, but the passengers near her tsked at her and gave her disapproving looks. She stuck her tongue out at one old man and then slipped into a seat. She pressed her face and hands to the window hoping he would see her too. He howled and chuckled inside of her head.

"Stay on the train until the last station. You'll be safe and warm that way. I'll meet you there."

Was he going to run all the way to the next station? Farther? Key glanced around to see if she could figure out where this train was going.

A white placard was screwed into the wall above the windows. It showed a line with periodic dots labeled with words she did not understand. One dot was lit up. That must be their next stop. The labels appeared to be city names. The last dot on the line was labeled *Praha Hlavni Nadrazi.*

Prague.

Huh. She'd always wanted to travel. This just wasn't how she thought her grand European adventure would go, but she also hadn't ever thought she'd have psychic powers or fall for a cranky wolf shifter.

Oh.

Ohhhh. Yeah. She was falling for Mik. Now what in the world was she going to do about that? She didn't want a wolf for a boyfriend, much less have to go through that whole mating ritual.

Although... she touched her shoulder where the old mark was. The sheriff had bit her to control her in all the wrong ways. He'd hurt her and cursed her with this special ability. But when Gal and Poppy, and all the other women who'd gotten mated to wolves were marked by their mates, they'd experienced pleasure, and embraced their gifts.

Someone who she assumed must be a train conductor walked toward her down the aisle. Crap. He would want to see her ticket. He stopped at another passenger and Kiara watched him tear off a slip of paper from a pad dangling from the belt at his waist and exchange it for money.

Yeah. This dress didn't have pockets so she couldn't even pretend to be searching for money to give him. She was just about to get up and see if she could sneak away to the bathroom or something, when another woman came and plopped down into the seat right next to her.

Ugh. It wasn't like the car was full. There were at least a dozen empty benches. She swiveled to give the lady a dirty look but instead forgot how to breathe. "Taryn?"

"Hiya, Key." She smiled and didn't flinch even a little as four enormous, fierce looking, super models sat down on the benches in front and behind her. "Meet my mates. This is August, Vasily, Grigori, and Joachim."

"Your mates, as in plural, as in all of them?" That was a lot of man... wolf... penises.

"Yeah. I'm a lucky girl that way." She blew a kiss in their direction. "Now, I need you to do me a favor."

"Did you know I would be here? What are you doing here?" This was super weird and very suspicious. She eyeballed the woman and decided it wasn't even truly the same one who'd gone missing last year. "What is going on Taryn? The last I heard you ran away."

"Yeah, long story, and I'll tell you when you get back to Rogue. I'm staying at the old Bay Inn. Heli and Kosta have fixed it up really nice."

Key tried to interject but Taryn just barreled over her.

"So, listen. I thought Jett could get this to the little red witch for me, but it turns out he's a bit preoccupied. The butthead. You'd think saving someone from Hell would entitle you to a couple of favors at least. You're going to have to deliver it for me. I really can't get involved."

Taryn handed Key a sheer trinket bag with a Christmas ornament shaped like one of those spiral seashells, with glitter, and a blue light inside.

What the hell?

Just up the aisle, the train conductor was caught up in a foot-tall swirling dust devil. The woman from the wedding reception was in the seat next to him, and Key gawked as she used his and the rest of the passengers' distracted state to tear off one of the paper tickets with a wave of her hand and floated it over to her seat.

The ticket taker pulled himself back together, brushed himself off, and glared at the others who were openly staring at him. He reached out his hand and to wedding reception woman and said, *"Bileta, prosim."*

She handed him her purloined ticket and then sank

into her seat, looking just as tattered and exhausted as Key. She should go to her. And say what? Compare demon war stories? Maybe not.

The ticket taker made his way down the row of benches, punching tickets, and finally over to her. Wait. Where did Taryn and her platoon of mates go? Key didn't even get to ask who this red witch was and how she was supposed to find her. Taryn was definitely in league with the Goddess of the Moon.

The man frowned at her appearance, looked at her bare feet and dress that was definitely worse for the wear. Oh geez. Was that a chunk of demon wyrm goo on her left boob?

"*Bileta, prosim.*"

She could only assume he was asking for her ticket. "Sorry, I don't understand Czech, and I don't..."

A small paper ticket with the same words as the final station, Praha Hlavni Nadrazi, printed on it was attached to the string on the ornament bag. She pulled it off and offered it to the train conductor. "Is this what you want?"

She held the piece of paper, praying it was valid. He punched it with his little hand-held machine and handed it back to her. Then he just walked away. Guess train conductors see some weird stuff.

Phew.

She spent the next twenty minutes staring at the placard waiting for the dot to change. The next stop on the line to Prague lit up. A chime and then a female voice came over a crackling loudspeaker saying a whole lot of k, ch, zh guttural sounds.

She heard that announcement four more times in the next hour and a half. She almost had the foreign words memorized by the time they rolled toward the final destination. *"Ukoncete prism, vystup a nasty, Deere se zaviraji."* Then finally, *"Pristi stanice Praha Hlavni Nadrazi."*

Next stop, Prague. They passed through some tunnels at the edge of the city, and she just about shredded the sheer bag with the ornament worrying it between her fingers, twisting it over and over. How Mik was going to stay hidden given that he was a big ass freaking wolf?

Dawn approached as they pulled into the station, and she made her way out through an already busy crowd of travelers. No way Mik was going to be able to find her with all these people around.

She walked outside to the small park in front of the station and thought maybe if she hung around the edges under some trees or something, but that wasn't going to work either.

"Stay where you are, pchelka. I'm coming to you now."

Key spun in a circle. No giant wolves were anywhere in her vicinity. There was a group of rowdy children coming her way though. Were they riding a shaggy horse? Oh gosh. It was Mik. They were riding on, and skipping alongside of him, coming straight for her.

No one walking about even took any notice of them. The group came right up to her, and she was instantly surrounded in noisy, frenetic little bodies. The ringleader, who'd been astride Mik, slid off, gave her a little bow, and said something that she was quite sure was an inappropriate flirtation.

Mik shoved his snout into her hand, and before she could even check to make sure no one was watching, he shifted into his human form. Ringleader smirked and shook his head, knowing he'd just been one-upped. Then he handed over a parcel that had a pretty worn pair of pants, a thin t-shirt, and some flip flops.

"Who are these kids and how do you have them under your spell? Also, this one just tried to pick my pocket." She gave the kid her best mom face, but the little girl shrugged.

"You are fair game, *pchelka*. These children are Romani. My people and theirs have a long, intertwined history. Their red witches are revered among many shifter communities. Most have shifter blood in them from the years before my people were forbidden from mating with humans, so they know a wolf shifter when they meet one."

"Whoa. What?"

"When the Children of the Moon left ancient Sumeria millenia ago—"

"No, I mean about them having red witches. I'm supposed to give this to a little red witch." She looked down at her pick pocket. "Is it you?"

The little girl shook her head and then bolted away. She didn't go far though. A woman with the most beautiful brown skin, and big emotive eyes, looking like she'd just walked off the cover of either Vogue or National Geographic with her billowy skirts, caught the girl up and lifted her into her arms.

"Where did you get that? There is a very powerful spell inside." She nodded toward the Christmas ornament, a wary look in her eyes.

"Umm, a friend on the train gave it to me." And then disappeared into thin air. "Do you know the little red witch?"

The woman scoffed. "Every Romani woman doesn't know every other. Do you know every Oracle in America?"

"Sorry. That was insensitive of me. I'm just anxious to get rid of this thing. It's pretty and all, but it gives me the heebie jeebies for some reason." Key leaned over to Mik and whispered, "Did she just call me an Oracle?"

He nodded. "I told you, they have a long history with the supernatural."

"Why don't you use your gift to find the red witch you're seeking." There was a definite surprised quality to her tone. Kind of like, duh.

Sigh. "Mine doesn't work that way. I spew out visions when they hit me upside the head. No control over it whatsoever."

The woman looked between Key and Mik and raised her eyebrow. "Because you have not allowed your mate to claim you. Why? What are you waiting for?"

PRIESTESSES AND PENISES

*H*e didn't want a mate, he'd decided that long ago. He was the last of the Volkov's true bloodline and with his death, there would be no more. He would not let another child be groomed into becoming a despot.

But he'd already died, and been reborn with a new purpose, a new life. Perhaps it was time to leave those old vows behind with his old life.

Mik placed his hand at the small of Kiara's back and guided her through the busy square. "Come with me, *pchelka*, the Goddess's task can wait for us to eat, rest, and regroup."

He had connections in Prague. People loyal to him that would be surprised as shit to see him in the flesh, seeing as he'd been dead for the better part of a year. He studied the nearest public transportation map and found the tram route he was looking for.

"Crap. We didn't already fulfill her task?"

His sweet, naive witch. They weren't off the hook so easily. "That ornament is from her. She did say that we would have multiple tasks. The first did not go according to her plan, so she has set us another."

Find a red witch that would have need of that spell. But why, to what end? Didn't really matter, but he didn't like the feeling of not being in control and continually used in the Goddess's games. No wolf had seen her in thousands of years. If she was interfering in mortal's lives now, there was a bigger reason.

When the tram towards *Vozovna Motol* pulled up, he waved Kiara to get on. Her eyebrows went up, but she took his hand, and they got on through the last set of doors. It was early enough that there weren't a whole lot of passengers yet. He gave the few who were seated at the back a scowl and the young men scurried to find new seats.

When they got settled, Kiara resumed their conversation in a quiet tone. "But a girl I used to know from back in Rogue gave this to me."

Interesting. So much of this intrigue was centered around the Troikas. "And where is she now?"

"Probably off getting railed by her four sex-on-a-stick mates." Key whispered that last part under her breath. "I don't know, she sort of disappeared."

The hair on the back of his neck stood up on end. "Did you say four mates?"

"Yeah, I know. That's a lot, right? That isn't just me. Like where do all those penises even go?"

He had to keep from snort laughing at that. Either she was being cute, or his witch was more inexperienced than he suspected. That would make for interesting bed games with her. He'd never been with anything but highly experienced submissives. He would need a tight rein on every bit of his control to ensure he didn't hurt her and brought her pleasure. Assuming she allowed him to. Even that was a new thought for him. He's always taken what he wanted. Now he wanted only what she would give him.

"That was definitely the Wolf Guard. They are the Goddess's High Priests, representing the phases of the moon. I assure you, she knows exactly where to put that many cocks."

Kiara's lashes fluttered as she considered his words. "Are priests even allowed to mate? Like, aren't sexy times forbidden for them or something?"

"That is a prescript of your modern-day human religion talking. Priests and priestesses of the ancient gods and goddesses were often pleasure mates just as much as religious figures." Even in the mating rituals of today, sex was an important part of the worship of the Goddess. Matings were consummated under the full moon, witnessed by their whole pack.

He and Kiara wouldn't have that.

She waggled her eyebrows at him. "That's kind of hot."

Oh Goddess. "Do you have a thing for the forbidden, my sweet?"

"Maybe. Do I? I think I do." She shot him a cheeky grin and that gave him all kinds of ideas. He was very much looking forward to exploring all her kinks and fantasies.

The tram took them across the Vltava River toward the Hradchany District to where the castle and St. Vitas Cathedral towered. Each time anyone even came close to the back of the tram, he growled and scared them off. The smart ones knew a predator when they saw one and never even approached the two of them.

"Come, this is our stop." They got off at Malostranska and he deftly led her through the small allies with old cobblestone streets to a secluded row of homes. Wolf shifters had long lived among the people of Prague in these same exact homes. He found the door he was looking for and pushed the buzzer.

A solid young man opened the door wearing a scowl similar to Mik's. "You're not welcome—"

"*Dzrastvie*, Eyrik."

The man stepped back, and his hand flew to his chest. "Misha? Have you come to haunt me for not being in Russia and protecting you as I should have?"

He fell to his knees and put his head to the floor. Kiara gasped quietly and squeezed Mik's hand. He probably should have warned her that he'd expected that kind of reaction. "No. You were a loyal and trusted guard. Let your conscience be clear that you did all that you could to keep me safe. Hell has no grip on you. Stand up and let us into your home. We seek sanctuary and rest from our journey here."

Eyrik rose and waved them in, taking a look up and down the alley before closing the door. He kept himself a distance away, clearly still afraid he was seeing a specter of the past. Mik couldn't blame him. "How is that you are here, my liege? You... you died."

Kiara looked at him sideways. "You did what now?"

"I did. But I was saved from the depths of Hell so I can seek vengeance." Mik's wolf pushed toward the surface, reveling in the remembered anger. Only Kiara's hold on him kept the beast at bay. "But first we need a place to rest, food, and clothing. I have no resources and will have to—"

"My liege, all that is mine is yours."

Mik put a hand on his friend and former guard's shoulder. "I am not the Wolf Tzar anymore. I am not back to reclaim that title, only to make those who betrayed me pay. Then my life is my own."

Eyrik didn't need to know they were also on a mission from the Goddess of the Moon. One revelation was enough for the day.

Eyrik eyed Kiara and gave a nod. "I... see. There is a bedroom with a bath at the top of the stairs. My closet has anything you will need. I will procure something for the lady."

He bowed and reached for Kiara's hand. Mik growled and Eyrik froze. "I wish only to thank the witch for saving you."

It took Mik a moment to reign his possessiveness over

Kiara in. "Your actions and words are enough. Do not touch her."

"Why does everyone keep calling me a witch? Did I grow some unexpected warts on my nose or something?" She grinned at Eyrik, trying to break the tension with a little soft flirting. Being smart man that he was, he took another step back.

"No, my lady, but you radiate power. If you're not a witch, you must be a Goddess." Eyrik's eyes drifted down, taking in Kiara's round belly, hips, thighs, and ass.

Yes, she did have the lusty figure of a Goddess, but that didn't mean any other man could ogle her. Mik stepped in between them. "Tell no one but your most trusted allies that I am here. But perhaps you should find a woman to help my mate, so you don't get yourself onto my shit list."

Kiara smacked him with her free hand. "Hey, you don't know that women wouldn't be lusting after me too, butthead."

Eyrik nodded and rushed away, out the door, leaving them to find the bedroom and bath. Mik dragged her straight into the shower, stopping only to set the Goddess's Christmas ornament on the sink. He needed to lose himself in her, know that she was safe, and his. After what the wise Romani mother said, he knew what he had to do. Whether she wanted him or not.

"You're right. I'm very sure men, women, and anyone with a beating heart would lust after you. But that doesn't mean I'll let them have a taste of what's mine."

He turned on the hot spray of the shower, despite them both being fully clothed. She wouldn't want this, and he would have to woo her with foreplay. That was not a particular skill of his. He stripped the tattered dress right over her head and tossed it onto the bathroom floor. Her bra and panties were next, and he shredded both with a deft couple of swipes of his claws.

"Hey. What if your friend can't find replacements in my size?" Kiara reached for his shirt and pulled it over his head and then went to work on the zipper and button of the trousers.

Fuck, her touch burned him in all the best ways. Perhaps she would be more enthusiastic about his claiming her than he thought. "I assure you, he has memorized your curves, as have I. He is no stranger to the large, round, and soft female form. He'll know what to get you. I trust him."

"No you don't. You literally put yourself between him and me downstairs." She shoved his pants down and he kicked them off. They'd waited far too long to indulge in each other's bodies, and he would use the emotions and their need to his advantage.

The hot water poured over them both and he ran his hands along the curve of her hips, up her sides and cupped her breasts. She gasped as she pinched her nipples between his thumb and fingers.

"You're right. I don't. I could scent his desire for you. But you're mine, and when I claim you, every other wolf will know you belong to me." He knew she didn't like his words, the implication that she was his property, but he would belong to her just as much as she to him.

"I... I..." She whimpered and turned her face away, her body betraying her mind. She did want him, but she was afraid. Afraid he would hurt her and ruin her life like the bastard who'd marked her.

"I know, *pchelka*."

"No... I..." Her eyes went white, and Mik felt the familiar constriction in his chest.

What the fuck was with these visions coming on when he was pleasuring her body? "Kiara, listen to me. You can control this. Grab onto the vision in your mind and see what it wants you to know."

She leaned into him, and while her body was rigid, her breathing didn't stop this time. The Romani woman had said that her power didn't work right because he hadn't claimed her. There was no more denying, even to each other, that they were mates.

Her past experience with being marked had been traumatic, and she might hate him afterwards, but he had to believe that by beginning the mating process, but marking her himself, it would help her now, caught in the whirlwind of her unbridled power.

He lowered his mouth to the crook of her neck and shoulder, catching the scent of the residual bond that piece of shit had left on her with his mark. He gently rubbed her back, soothing her, as he scraped his teeth across the tattoo-like scribble of another man's wolf mark. He could literally taste the weak and foul toxicity of what that bastard had done to her.

If Mik was to erase the damage on her soul, he would need to bite deep, cutting out the blight, and replacing it with his own spirit. But was that any better?

Kiara's fingernails dug into his back, and she trembled in his arms, still unable to speak or move. It was now or never. Mik let the portion of the wolf that he'd wrestled control of surge up, and he sank his teeth deep into her flesh.

The vision in her mind flooded into his and suddenly the two of them were dancing, swirling around to well-practiced steps, in a ballroom of sorts. He wore a military uniform of old, and she, a billowy dress and powdered hair. The room was lit by candlelight alone, and the music came from instruments little played in the modern age.

As the steps came to a close and the music wound down, he pulled her aside, pushed her against the wall, just as he'd done back in her small home a few days ago. He breathed in her ripe peach scent and growled, pressing his lips to the same spot where his teeth lay buried in real life. He kissed the spot, then kissed her, so deeply, they both were lost in the lust. He broke the kiss, gasping. "You're mine, Princess. Those Habsburg wolves cannot have you."

She leaned into him, and her rosy cheeks went even pinker. "I am already betrothed to Hartmann. Our marriage will bring peace between Bohemia and Germany."

Never. She belonged to him now and forever. "I will kill him rather than let him claim you."

The image faded and he was back in the shower with Kiara. He pulled his teeth from her shoulder and licked over the deep wound he'd made. Already the false mark was fading under the darker, inky black of his wolf forming in its place.

"Ow," Kiara said, but didn't let him go, or even slap him. "But also... can you do that again? I think I missed the good part."

The aroma of her utter arousal mixed with the satis-faction of sexual release floated on the steam swirling around them. "Sweet witch, I think we both missed the good part."

"I promise to do this all over again, when we can both enjoy every bit of it." His bite and marking had made her come, but she wasn't the only one. His seed was spread across her belly and dripped down her thighs where the water had splashed down from his body. He reached between them, smearing the pure essence of him across her skin, drawing it down between her thick, luscious thighs.

He wanted to see her come for him, wanted to stroke his cock along her wet skin until they were both ready for him to push her down, making her submit to him, as he properly claimed her body, mind, and soul.

It took every bit of control he had, but he turned off

the hot water, grabbed the fluffy towel off the heating rack, and wrapped her up in it. Then he lifted her into his arms princess style and carried her into the bedroom. On the bed were two parcels, wrapped in brown paper and string, as well as a tray with bottles of water, bread, cheese, sliced meats, and pickles.

He tucked her against the pillows and crawled in beside her. She reached for the tray and built them both bite size sandwiches out of the fixings. "I feel different than before, like something that was keeping me bound tight has undone."

Mik grabbed a slice of cheese and pressed it against her lips. She opened for him, and he fed her the morsel. "The mark of the wolf who hurt you is gone."

Kiara reached up and touched her shoulder. "Replaced by yours?"

"Yes." He would not apologize for that.

"I think I'm supposed to be mad at you for that." She frowned, and a whole myriad of thoughts flashed through her eyes. "There's a lot of things I'm sure I'm supposed to feel around you."

Yes. She should be scared, angry, irritated, scared again. Yet here she was snuggled up in his arms, replete, calm, satisfied, content. "Your power is wrapped up in your emotions. Harness those, and you'll have a handle on your visions."

The took a bite of her sandwich and made a hmm-ing sound. He wasn't sure if it was because of the good food or acknowledging what he'd said.

AIDY AWARD

"That's the first time I've seen one of my own visions. But that one didn't have the future. We were in the past. Did that mean something to you?"

Mik didn't think that vision was meant for him, or not him alone. With the control she'd arrested, perhaps she could also finally use her power for herself too. "I know where that vision took place. Right here, at Prague Castle."

Kiara dropped her sandwich and her towel. "Then we need to go there. Now. Right now."

"You need rest, and to finish your food."

"Mikhail, there is something important at that castle. We'll eat on the way, and sleep when we're dead." She made an oh-shit face that made him laugh. "Sorry. Do people even sleep when they're dead? I guess you would know."

"I can definitely say that I did not sleep in Hell."

"Huh. Okay, well, then we can sleep tonight. After we go see what in the world the Goddess wants us to discover at the castle. Come on, let's go. Get these clothes on your way too good-looking body before I change my mind and jump your bones."

He'd rather option B, but for the first time in this life or the last, he wasn't in charge, and her wish was his command. He liked it that way.

DEJA VIEW

*E*ver since she was bitten and controlled by one really bad wolf shifter, Key had been angry and afraid. She tried really hard not to be. She put on a brave face, went to therapy, smiled a lot even when she didn't feel like it, and pushed her fear and rage down as deep as it could go.

She thought if she put those emotions away in a dark corner of her mind and ignored them, they'd die like plants with no light or water. Turned out they were more like tulip bulbs than creeping ivy, because they were just lying in wait for their chance to push up into any shred of light.

Killing that demon with her shoe had done more for her than a year of therapy. Letting Mik bite her and mark her? It hadn't taken all of her fear away, no. It had taken that fear, watered it, put it out in the sunlight, let it grow until she thought it would completely take over and strangle her...

Until she paid attention to the soft way he stroked her back, the groan of his own need overwhelming him but doing nothing about it, and the fact that he literally sucked away the bad wolf's disgusting mark so she wouldn't suffer under its taint any longer.

When Key leaned into him and the way he was trying so hard to protect her when he himself was broken too, that's when the fear was truly crushed. Each of those vines of panic and dread withered and were crushed under the connection of their two souls.

That's when the vision came.

She still didn't have complete control, but at least she got to see it this time. For the first time ever, her vision was for and about her. She didn't even know that was a possibility. Once she understood there was a Goddess that had created wolf shifters, she assumed these visions were a way for her to communicate with her people. Almost all of her prophecies or whatever they were had been for either wolves or their mates.

Even her very first one had been about the return of Niko, who was now the Wolf Tzar.

Did that mean that Key was now one of the Goddess's children? She was just a plain old human before the attack. She'd felt like a broken, awkward plain old human after.

Not special.

Just... cracked in ways that couldn't be fixed.

Faster than she could imagine, Mik was filling in those cracks. They would never go away, but they could be healed. That was the miracle of falling in love.

Yep. Great googly mooglies, she was in love with Mikhail Volkov, a big, grumpy, possessive, alpha wolf-shifter. The last thing she ever thought could or would happen to her.

She gripped Mik's hand tighter as they walked toward the castle, and he gave her a squeeze back. He'd been quieter since their sexy times turned marking turned vision in the shower. He hadn't said, but the vision had affected him even more than it had her. Because he knew where it had taken place. He remembered.

Eyrik led them up an entirely too long pathway that was steep enough, stairs had been set into it every three feet or so. The walkway wound around the cliff-like wall of the back and side of Prague Castle.

"It's not cheating to let us in this back gate without getting tickets?" She expected to see a lot more visitors to such a huge tourist destination, but there was hardly anyone around. The day was a little chilly, but not so much that people wouldn't come out sight-seeing.

"No, my lady. My family has guarded this castle and the royals who lived here for generations. I know who belongs here and who doesn't." He nodded to them both. "You belong. As does Misha."

"I don't really see how. Just because I had a vision of being here a long time ago?" She had psychic powers, sure. But that didn't mean she belonged here, thousands of miles away from home.

"No, *pchelka,* because if I'm right about what we saw in your vision, you are in fact a royal."

"Don't be silly." She half snort-laughed. "My family is from New Jersey."

"Hmm." He raised one eyebrow, not agreeing with her, but not saying so either. "Let's just see what's what when we get to the castle."

"We're here." Eyrik gave a small two-fingered salute to soldier in a blue uniform with red and white cord and tassels standing guard. The soldier didn't even acknowledge them, and that was probably a good thing.

He let them into the grounds through a black wrought iron gate, on the side of the public entrance. The further into the castle complex they got, the harder Key's heart beat. She placed her free hand over her chest and could literally feel the pounding against her palm.

Eyrik stopped at the bottom of a long, bricked ramp that gently sloped with six platformed step ups, enclosed with a ceiling decorated in swirling trusses. As she looked toward the end of this hallway, she had to blink twice, because she swore there were horses clip-clopping toward them.

Mik pulled her closer. "Thank you, Eyrik, I think we know where to go from here."

The crazy thing was, she did know where to go. This weird horse rider's hallway felt so familiar that it was almost eerie. She'd never even been to Europe. much less

Prague or this castle. Her whole life had been spent in and around the Rogue area. She didn't even have a passport.

But she also had definitely been here before.

They were both quiet as they climbed the long ramp with the stairs set quite low so horses could maneuver them, and her heart fluttered, sending ripples up and down her ribs, the closer they got to the dark curtains cordoning off the room on the other side. Mik stepped forward and pushed one of the draperies aside, and the light shined so brightly, she had to blink while her eyes adjusted.

She stepped into a great hall and whoosh, an almost euphoric sense of home wrapped around her. "Mik, I've been here before. Like, right here, where we're standing right now."

Key wasn't only seeing the room around her, there was also a courtyard, and different buildings. "I think I'm seeing hundreds of years of this place all at the same time."

"I know. I was here with you through it all." While his tone was still confident and self-assured like the alpha that he was, for the first time, she heard wonder in his voice.

"What we saw this morning, and even now, it's more than just my visions for us both, isn't it? Something more like memories, I think." Key had never really believed in anything paranormal before she'd been bitten, and that included reincarnation. But there was no denying that her sense of knowing this place as well as she knew her own home, but over hundreds and hundreds of years, was undeniable.

"It absolutely was. We have both been here before. Lifetime after lifetime. We've come together here. This place is... ours somehow." He glanced around the room as if searching for an answer to what they were seeing and experiencing. "I don't understand why this is being shown to us now, but this has to be the work of the Goddess."

Was the Goddess here now?

She and Mik were almost the only visitors in this part of the castle. There was just one other woman slowly strolling along the carpet runner placed along the outside edge of the great hall. The wooden floor in the center was cordoned off with polished gold posts draped by puffy ropes between them to keep people out. Key already knew exactly what it was like to walk across that floor, dance around and around on it even.

Then there were those four enormous, very familiar-looking guards standing at each corner of the room. The one nearest to them gave a casual jerk of his forehead toward the other end of the room as if to tell them that was where they should go next.

Mik didn't even acknowledge the woman or the guards. He kept walking across the room as if they were the only ones here. He wasn't even admiring the gothic vaulted ceilings, or the way sunlight poured in exactly in the spots where the market stalls would have been set up so that the occupants of the castle grounds could buy and sell their goods.

Key could almost hear the vendors bargaining for a few coins more, smell the horses and the food and the people, she could taste the mulling spices for winter wine in the air.

Would the whole castle have this same intense deja vu feeling? If she thought about it for a moment, she realized there would be a side room with a big, green ceramic tiled stove to keep it warm in the winter, and big windows to keep it cool in the summer. Someone had once been thrown out one of those windows.

As they walked past the other woman visitor who was consulting a guidebook, she glanced at them with a smile. "I hear the princess had a lavish bedroom upstairs where she would sneak in her lover, and that's why her engagement was called off."

Holy Roman Emperors, how did she know?

The windowed rooms were indeed off the side at the front of the hall, but just inside and to the left was a large stone staircase... that led to the rooms upstairs. Rooms she had lived in. Rooms she'd invited Mik into even though she was betrothed to another.

Mik opened the short metal gate across the stairs that read - Do Not Enter, Authorized Personnel Only in several languages - and led her through, and then quickly up the staircase. She looked behind to make sure no one saw. Just like she'd done hundreds of years before. No one had caught them then, and no one was around to see them enter this off-limits part of the Old Royal Palace now either.

At the top was a long hallway that spanned the length of the long room below. There were doors on each side and Key pointed to one not far from them. "That one."

Anticipation danced across her skin like the butterflies in her stomach had gotten out and were flapping their wings all up and down her arms, legs, breasts, and belly. She knew what the room should look like. A fireplace at one side, a big canopy-style bed against the wall, a vanity with a polished silver mirror and a jug of water and a porcelain basin to wash up in. It had later been used as land offices, and she had no idea what they would find in there now.

Together they pushed the door open and walked into an empty room, save an old but plush carpet on the floor. Her heart sank a bit, disappointed that there was nothing special here.

"Look up, my love."

Carved into the stone was a circle made up of the phases of the moon. In the center was the silhouette of a wolf howling against a full moon, surrounded by a field of stars dotted like the ancient night sky. Key's bite mark pulsed against her skin, and she reached up to touch it.

Mik's hand was already there, shoving her shirt aside. "It's my mark, here on your skin, and there on the ceiling. They're identical."

He bent his head and gently kissed the mark on her and the moon and stars on the ceiling illuminated. The room went dark as if it was midnight, but with the glowing of the moon above, a circle, sacred and divine lit up around them.

"Kiara, I'm not used to having to ask for what I desire, and I know you're afraid of me, but I promise to cherish and protect you with everything that I am. Will you allow me to claim you as my mate, here and now in this sacred circle the Goddess has provided for us?"

Marked.

Claimed.

Mated.

Nothing she ever wanted. Not after the way she was so violently thrust into the supernatural world that existed in secret all around her.

The idea of belonging to another had always been abhorrent. She was her own woman, reliant on no one. But look where that had gotten her. Scared, alone, and pretending to be happy, to be okay with her life.

"I didn't want to admit it, but I belonged to you, and you to me, the moment you walked into my life. I'm not afraid of you, I never was. I'm tired of being scared of everything else in my life. You're the first thing in a long time that makes me feel safe."

Mik swallowed hard and bowed his head. "I don't know how or why the fates decided I was ever worthy of you. But thank the Goddess, they did."

He pulled her into his arms and scraped his teeth across the mark, sending all the best kind of shivers all up and down her spine. "I claim you, Kiara Cross, princess of my heart. I claim you and take you for my mate."

"Just remember, you big bad wolf," Key held his mouth to her skin and let her heart open, a special kind of soul deep magic filling her and tumbling over into him and the room. "You belong to me, as much as I belong to you, now, in our pasts, and forever."

IF HE DIES, HE DIES

Mik might be angry at those who'd betrayed him, angry at the Goddess for using him, and angry at himself for losing all of his control over his own shift, but Kiara's love for him in this magical moment swept all of that away and replaced it with such intense emotions he couldn't even name them.

He could only feel and rely on his senses to show him the way to please her, touch her, taste her, claim her. The wolf inside howled to get out and with the little bit of control he had, he let it rise up in his mind. She wasn't afraid of him. Even when he was afraid of himself.

The human side of him said to be gentle with her, but the beast's instincts needed to dominate her, make her submit to him and his body so she knew exactly who was claiming her. He was the alpha, she was his mate.

The two of them had been drawn together in love, and then torn apart in lifetime after lifetime. The vision she'd had of them dancing had been only one where they'd claimed each other, and she'd been taken from him, forced to marry another. That had been true for a very long time. Lifetimes even.

He belonged to her as much as she belonged to him, and the machinations of wolves and men could never change that. This wasn't the first time he'd claimed her in this very spot. This magic flowing around them was ancient, as old as time, and deep in his soul, Mik knew that their love was just as old.

The Romani woman had seen something in them that they hadn't understood. They were both cursed with broken gifts from the Goddess, and with every part of his cracked soul, he knew absolutely that mating Kiara here and now would break those curses.

Would claiming her reveal the larger, darker curse that tore them apart in lifetime after lifetime? He would risk his own life to be with her, but he'd vowed to protect her.

Even as he hesitated, the light of the moon over their heads beamed down and illuminated her skin. She glowed for him and only him, as only a true mate would. He may not know what would happen after their mating, but he wouldn't deny either of them the chance to love and be loved in return any longer.

Curses could come, and they would deal with them then. Now was for sex, claiming, and love.

Mik kissed the mark on her neck and shoulder and this time, he let go of all his anger and fear. He finally gave in to the pure need for her. "Take off your new clothes, Kiara. My control is at an end, and I will shred them if you aren't naked and in my arms soon."

He stepped away, holding on to only a few strands of her hair to keep him from shifting. The wolf wanted out. Not this time.

Kiara smiled at him and melted away any remaining inhibitions. She slowly undid the buttons of her jacket and let the arms slide off, dropping it to the floor.

This was going to take an eternity, and the anticipation was far too delicious. The only thing holding him back from ripping the rest of her clothes off her body was the almost ritualistic way she removed her clothes. Each movement looked practiced, even though it couldn't have been. The way she kept her gaze directly on his eyes, never wavering, as if this was all an important part of a ceremony.

Kiara's eyes went white, but her body didn't tense, or freeze like before. His mind flashed back to another castle made of mud and sand, millenniums older, where another version of Kiara did this same ritualistic undressing for him under a desert moon. An ancient princess, preparing to become his wife.

As that vision faded, she said, "We've belonged to each other even longer than I could have imagined."

And something had kept them apart in life after life. That would end this time. She was his for all eternity. He would protect her, keep her safe, and not let anything or anyone take her from him again.

AIDY AWARD

"Yes. You have been mine for thousands of years. But it took my death for me to find you this time. I'm not letting you go again."

She pulled the jeans she wore down her legs and kicked them away. She was nearly naked, and the way her skin glowed so brightly had his wolf howling inside. Praising her as if she was the moon itself. She reached her arms around her back to undo her bra, but Mik stopped her.

"Let me."

He turned her around so that she faced away and instead of just unclasping the bra, he pulled the cups down, letting her breasts spill out, supported only by the underwire. He cupped the weight of them in his hands and rubbed his thumbs over her nipples until they beaded hard against his fingers.

Kiara leaned back against him and writhed under his touch. She ground her ass against his cock as if he wasn't already constantly hard for her. He was this close to shoving her to her knees, grabbing her hips, and thrusting into her to complete their joining.

He would make this good for her too, not just himself like the selfish asshole he used to be. If she was going to drive him crazy while he was still fully clothed, he was going to take advantage of the fact that she was nearly naked. Nearly.

He slid one hand down over the soft round of her belly and to the silky material of her panties. He wanted to slip his hand inside of them and into her slick cunt, but that would be too easy for them both. Instead, he stroked her through the material, teasing her, teasing them both. "Do you want me to fuck you hard and fast, bringing us both to climax and giving us relief from this damn tension we've been building for days?"

"Yes," she gasped out the word as he circled her clit but didn't touch.

"Or do you want me to take you slow and deep, so that neither of us know where I end and you begin?"

"Yes. Both. I want everything from you." Kiara arched her back and wrapped her arm around the back of his neck. "Give me all of you."

No one but her had ever wanted all of him. They wanted the leader, the dominant, the Wolf Tzar. The Volkovs had wanted a pawn, a biddable puppet. He was none of those things with her. She saw and loved the whole of him, filth and sin, caring and soul. All.

That's what he would give her.

He shifted his claws and sliced through the panties but left the shreds on her body. "On your hands and knees, now."

She whimpered at his demand and the scent of both her arousal and excitement filled the air like spiced fruit. Like the offerings of a priestess to her God of long ago.

Mik sank behind her and placed his hands on her spine, sliding them toward her shoulders, pushing her chest and face down so she was supplicating herself to the throne of their consummation. This was how he wanted to worship her body.

He spread her knees with his and reached between her legs where the shredded material of her panties stretched, failing to cover her wet and warm cunt any longer. He held her down with one hand and slid two fingers into her with the other. "This is mine. I'm claiming your soul and your body for my own."

She clenched around him and moaned, pushing back against him, sinking his fingers deeper. "I'm yours. I'm yours."

He stroked in and out, preparing and opening her for his cock. He wasn't small, and she was so tight. It would take more than a little foreplay for her body to take him. She needed to come so that her body relaxed. "Don't move, unless I tell you to. Got it?"

"Yes."

Mik laid down on the floor and flipped so his head and shoulders were between her legs. He grabbed her around the waist. "Up on your knees now. I want your cunt on my face so that I can taste you as you come in my mouth."

Kiara's legs shook, and for a moment, he thought she was either too turned on or he'd frightened her with his harsh demands. But there was no scent of fear from her. Then he realized she was giggling.

She sat up as he instructed, but stayed up too high. She looked down with a funny smirk on her face. "Are you sure? No one's ever asked me to do that before. Probably because I'll suffocate you with my thighs and fupa."

Her thighs, belly, and fat pussy lips were what made

her body so enticing to him in the first place. She had everything he desired in a feminine body. Built like the goddesses of old, and that turned him the fuck on. Of course he wanted her on his face.

He wrapped his hands around her ass and pulled her core to his mouth, positioning her clit in line with his tongue. Her giggles turned back into moans. He sucked on her clit rhythmically and flicked her tongue over it, lashing the little bud until her legs were shaking for all the right reasons.

"Oh God, Mik, I... I can't... I..." Her hips jerked in the tiniest of thrusts and he knew what she needed.

Without letting her get away, he slid his hands from her ass to her hips and helped her body thrust against him, riding his chin, lips, and face. That did the trick, and her moans turned higher in pitch until she exploded, her tight clit throbbing in his mouth and her cunt clenching as the orgasm flooded through her. He lapped at her, drawing out every last trembled beat of her climax, savoring the taste of her pleasure.

His cock ached against the fabric of his jeans, and he let it. He would get his own release soon enough, but not yet. This was a moment he wanted to revel in.

Kiara sank back and stared down at him, her eyes dark with satisfaction and lust. The look on her face was better than anyone else's he'd ever given an orgasm to. Her face erased all the others he'd been with forever. There was only her.

She let out a long, slow sigh and her muscles everywhere relaxed. That's exactly what he was waiting for. With a quick flip, he picked her up and laid her beneath him. His wolf howled that the claiming should be with her submitting to him, ass in the air, but Mik would not forgo seeing her face as she came on his dick.

This wasn't the Goddess's ritual. Their sacred circle was created from carvings in a castle, not a forest under the full moon. They had no pack to witness his claiming of her. Their mating was something special, and it would be the way they wanted and needed it to be.

This time Mik didn't have to push her knees open, she was ready for him. Kiara's body welcomed his, ready, waiting, and more than willing to be fucked. He tugged his t-shirt over his head and finally ripped open the fastening to the jeans and pushed them down. She reached for him and ran her nails down his chest, sending tingles across his skin.

"I claim you, Kiara, as my mate. You belong to me, and I to you, forever more." He leaned over her and positioned his cock at her entrance. In a slow and steady thrust, he went deep, letting her wet cunt take all of him. The bulge of his wolf's knot already swelled and the barest touch of her pussy lips against that sensitive part of him had his hips jerking and his wolf howling to come already.

"Yes, Mikhail. Take me, make me yours." She wrapped her heels around his ass and together they set up a hard rhythm. He took her in deep, penetrating strokes, pounding into her, fucking her hard.

She didn't take her eyes off his for even a second, but they did fill with the telltale white of her visions. "Stay with me, Kiara. This moment is ours alone."

Her eyes fluttered shut and she took gasping breaths, one for each of his thrusts into her body. "That's it, *pchelka*, feel my cock inside of you, feel what you do to my body, my mind. Use that to control your power and stay with me."

His balls ached, his wolf howled, and his knot throbbed, but he would not come until she was here in this moment with him. They would come together, and break both of their curses. "Come on, Kiara. You're mine, your body, and your mind. I want you with me. Now, Kiara."

He fucked her with everything he had, willing her to take him, all of him, just as she said she wanted. She was trying. Her eyes opened, clear, pupils blown, but seeing him again and not some vision. But she needed something more to defeat this curse. Her lips moved and she tried to speak, but the sounds weren't words.

He let his wolf rise up and connected his mind to hers, letting the meaning filter in through their connection. *"Tell me what you need, Kiara."*

"All of you. The good and the bad, the light and the dark. Let go of whatever you're holding back. I want all of you."

The good and the bad. The light and the dark. The man and the wolf.

Mik slipped his hand into her hair and tugged hard, exposing her throat to him. He howled and let the wolf rise up, not shifting, but letting the beast take over. He sunk his fangs into her skin, imbuing his mark with every bit of his true self and let the knot in his cock swell and expand until it felt so good it hurt.

"Mine." The word was little more than an animalistic growl, but her body responded and with his next thrust, her body took his knot and didn't let go. Mik roared out his release, shooting his seed deep into her cunt, marking every part of her with his scent, his claim.

Her pussy clenched around him, and she cried out his name and her own claim. "I claim you, Mikhail. I claim you as my mate."

ATTITUDE OF GRATITUDE

$\mathcal{K}$ ey floated in the bliss of really fucking great sex. Like mind blowing. Literally.

Something strange had happened to her brain, her psychic ability, her curse. When Mik had demanded that she stay with him she'd been trying to do exactly that, but couldn't. They were mid-claiming, fucking each other's brains out, and the power had done everything it could to pull her out of the moment.

She didn't get it. Only a few minutes before, she felt a vision come on, and had been able to show it to him and stay present.

But that had been a vision of herself, or rather the two of them together in some ancient time. Sort of like when they were in the shower and he'd marked her. That vision had been of them too, and that was the first time she'd even been able to see her own psychic ability at work.

It was the damn visions for or about other people that she couldn't control. It was fricking chaos and she hated it.

If he hadn't connected their minds, she would have been a goner. And that was one orgasm she didn't want to miss. But when he finally let go and released the control he was trying to hold over both of them, given up that last bit of self to her, he pulled her back from the void of nothing she was being sucked into head first.

Hell yeah.

That was something to be grateful for.

Mik. He was something she could truly be happy about. Not pretend happy like she'd been acting for years. Even before the sheriff's bite, she'd been faking it to make it. The feelings she had with Mik were all her, all real. Maybe for the first time in her life.

So whoever was fucking that up for her, could go eat a bag of rubber chicken penises. The squeaky ones.

You know, *after* she and Mik had all the orgasms they could handle. He was still buried deep inside her and she wouldn't have it any other way. She'd had sex, but not like this. Nothing like this. In fact, she could no longer even remember the names of her former partners.

There was only him. And his big old dick.

She'd never felt so full in all the best ways.

He also still had his fangs buried in the crook of her neck. That too felt weirdly good. She'd be all kinds of sore tomorrow, but it would be worth it.

Key stroked Mik's back, because while she was totally

with it, he wasn't. He'd allowed the wolf to rise up and take over part of his mind. He'd needed to in order to complete the claiming. At first, she thought he hadn't been able to because of whatever it was that she did to him when she touched him and forced him to shift into his human form. But once they'd connected their minds, she could feel the reticence within him. He had a tight control over the animalistic part of himself in order to not hurt her.

He was so sweetly protective of her. But she didn't need him to protect her from the wolf. She wanted all of him. The good and the bad. The man and the animal. The man and the freaking sex god. "Mikhail, my sweet wolf, are you okay?"

He grunted but lifted his head from her neck and licked over the new wound he'd made. Her skin tingled and she literally felt the fibers of her body knit back together. Ooh. Fancy wolf healing. Gal had gotten the ability to shift into a wolf after Max claimed her. Maybe Key would too. That would definitely make her feel more a part of both the community and Mik's life.

But if she was going to be a wolf shifter, wouldn't she already have at least felt the animal within her? Even now, with a very open mind about, there was no wild animal poking around the inner recesses of her consciousness. She could sense her psychic ability, like a weird, warpy, tye-died hippy flitting about her brain. But no wolf.

"I think I'm the one who is supposed to be asking you

that." Mik shifted so less of his weight was on her, but he did not pull out. She didn't mind. It was comforting to still have their bodies wrapped around each other, to be connected with him so intimately.

"Oh, I'm just fantastic, thank you very much. Have you always been that good in bed?" She teased, but his face went serious.

"Only with you." He moved his hips ever so slightly and, whoo boy, did she see stars, and moons, and some more stars. Maybe even some planets.

She gasped and wiggled her hips in response. "Whatever you just did, do it again."

Mik chuckled and pressed himself against her, making her eyes roll back in her head in the best way. "That's the wolf's knot, sweet bee. Until the beast is satisfied you are well claimed, we will remain connected together. I can't pull out from your body even if I wanted to."

"What? Like, really?" She found this idea both thrilling and super weird. "Why did none of the other mates ever tell me this? There should be a book on how to mate with a shifter."

"Yes. Now that the Troikas have claimed human females as their true mates, that kind of manual would come in useful on both sides of the supernatural. I was worried I would hurt you, but you seem to be enjoying all I have to give you." He thrust the teensiest bit and they both moaned.

Just because they were stuck together didn't mean

they couldn't have some fun. Key slid her hands down his powerful back and squeezed his butt. He growled in the most delicious way that sent those butterflies swirling all along her skin, through her lower belly, and right between her legs.

He waggled his eyebrows at her. "I bet I could make you come again simply by growling at you."

"Yep. That and your magic penis. You're way better than any vibrator."

Mik did indeed growl at that, and with only a few small movements that couldn't be called much more than a nudge, she was bucking against him and panting his name.

"That's it, *pchelka*, let me feel your cunt squeeze my knot as you come on my cock again. Come for me, grip my knot tight inside of your body." He made each word a demand, and in his huskiest voice, made especially for her.

What could she do but happily comply?

What? Like it was hard to have another orgasm when he was talking dirty to her and hitting all the right places with both his dick and his big dick energy? Nope. That was easy peasy pussy squeezy.

Her muscles locked as the orgasm hit her, and somewhere in the hazy delight, she realized the sensations in her muscles were similar to when a vision was barreling its way through her too. No wonder her body was so fricking confused.

"Aw, fu-uck, Kiara." He pressed his forehead to hers.

"I'm never leaving your body. We are going to have to live out our lives in this stone room and perish from dehydration as I give you every last drop of seed I have."

"Fine by—" she closed her eyes just for a moment and when she opened them again, Mik was no longer on top of her or inside of her. He had her cradled in his lap, stroking her hair, and whispering softly to her.

"Dammit." She threw her head back and her arms out to the side in a full-on tantrum. Mik pulled her deeper into his arms, comforting her the best he could in her frustration. "A vision? I thought I was starting to get a handle on them."

"Yes. As did I, but this one seemed to slam into you with a force unlike the others, yet was directed to me." Mik's tone had taken a turn toward the dark, and not in the sexy way.

"What's wrong?" She did not like the flash of fear that went through his eyes so fast, she would have missed it if she wasn't so focused on him. "What did I say?"

"Nothing. It isn't important." He tried to look away, but she grabbed his chin and brought his gaze right back to hers.

"Mikhail Volkov, don't you think you can keep anything from me. Not after what just happened between us. We are together till the end. You hear me?" He wanted her to let her anger out more? This was something she could get angry about.

He pulled her hand from his face and pressed a kiss to her palm. Then he sighed and looked up at the ceiling.

The moon and stars were still there in the carvings, but the room was no longer illuminated, and their skin wasn't glowing anymore either. "I told you mad was a sexy look on you. I enjoy it far too much when you chastise me like that."

She put on her best growl for him this time. "Mikhail."

"Yes, exactly like that love. If you hadn't just scared the hell out of me, I'd be hard again in a second and have you on your hands and knees for me."

"Stop avoiding the question. What did I say?" As long as she'd known him, in this life and all their previous lives that she'd caught glimpses of, he didn't avoid danger. He headed straight into it. For funsies. So it was making her really nervous the way he was skirting the question with flirting.

"It was nothing more than an invitation back to Hell." He waved it off with a shake of his head.

Oh, was that all? Just Hell waiting on them. Where was that guidebook to the supernatural when she needed it? She was talking someone into writing it when they got back to Rogue. Like Gal or Poppy. They were librarians, they knew everything about books and werewolves and possibly even Hell if she'd ever thought to ask about it. If they ever made it back to Rogue. Until then, it was the two of them against the world. Or against Hell.

She was going to ask him something she really didn't want to. He wasn't going to like it either, but it was well beyond time they stopped reacting to everything happening to them and took some action. "I think you need to tell me what happened when you... died."

"Yes, I do." He stroked her hair and looked right through her. "I want you to tell me about when you were first bitten."

Gulp. At least they were on the same wavelength. "You think that's relevant?"

"Yes. The more we learn, the more I think there is more underlying our plight than we realize." He narrowed his eyes, studying some bit of information in his own head. "Someone or something has been fighting to keep us from each other. Not only in this lifetime, but in the past. Each time I find you, we're later torn apart. Why?"

"Could someone also be working for us?" She didn't really know anything about the Goddess of the Moon, but being a goddess and all had to come with some pretty spectacular powers. She certainly had a vested interested in the two of them. "No one else I know in the supernatural community has ever said anything about reincarnation or that they find each other in multiple lives."

Mik cupped her face and brushed his lips across her so tenderly that it was hard to think straight. "I have every reason to believe that is the power of our love for each other. I will always find you. You will always be mine."

The few visions she'd had that were her own, where she'd seen the two of them together, had her thinking that if she could break this curse that made it so she went all catatonic and blurted out prophecies and things, perhaps the underlying power was her own. She'd hoped truly mating with Mik would do the trick, but she'd just had another episode so there was something else she had to figure out.

"Do you have any idea when we first fell in love?" Both of her visions of them were from times long gone, but he seemed to know more about them than she did. "The time we were dancing was here in the castle around medieval times, but the other felt a lot older and somewhere outside of Europe."

"Wolf lore says that the first children of the moon were created in ancient Sumer when the worshippers of Ningal were attacked by demons... from Hell." He nodded as the pieces of the puzzle began to fall into place. "The Goddess gave us the gift of shifting into wolves to defend ourselves against the demons. I have a feeling our love goes back as far as those first people."

Except for one thing. "I don't shift. A lot of the other mates do. But there is a group that only get some kind of psychic gifts. No one has quite figured out who will shift and who won't. Everyone who has, learns to shift pretty quickly."

"You don't think you're a child of the moon." It wasn't a question.

"In the second vision, it looked and felt like a ritual. You said people worshipped gods and goddesses back then. Could I have been some kind of priestess for some other god or goddess?"

"Of course. The Sumerians worshipped many gods and goddesses. But then how did we end up together?"

"Clearly, we weren't supposed to." Key trembled from head to toe and back again. "If our love was sanctioned, would someone be trying so hard to keep us apart that they have to work across time and space?"

THE WHIMS OF GODS AND GODDESSES

*N*o way in hell—heh, Kiara's snarky sense of humor and sunshiny version of rage was rubbing off on him. But—no way in hell was he going back to Hell, and he certainly wasn't bringing his mate with him.

The dragons could solve their own damn problems. Or if they couldn't, the Goddess could choose someone else to help her get to this all-powerful witch trapped in Ereshkigal's realm. Why the fuck she didn't just pop down there and get the girl herself was a mystery he didn't care to solve.

And, if this Red Witch was so powerful, why didn't she come on up here and do whatever spell she was going to do to save dragonkind or whatever?

He was done.

And so was Kiara.

They had better things to do with their time than the errands of gods and goddesses. Who the fuck did these all-mighty beings think they were to interfere in the lives of mortals? Fuckers.

Kiara was right. They were going to stop reacting to what the Goddess and Hell wrought upon them, and take back their lives, their control over their own lives. Starting now.

First, to see if their mating had broken his curse as he hoped it would. Then, they would go about solving the mystery of hers. "Let's see if I can control my shift. You go get your clothes."

"The ones you didn't shred, you mean. I liked these panties. You were right, Eyrik did know what would suit me."

Mik helped her to her feet, and then gave her a swift swat on the ass for even thinking about another man. She giggled. Outright bubbly giggled. Even with the red imprint of his hand on her flesh. They would be trying a lot of new kinks in their bedplay. And he knew a lot of kinky ass games.

Her shirt and trousers were halfway across the room and the further away she got, the more his skin and bones tingled. Shit. She dropped the shredded panties to the floor and then bent to pick up the clothes, showing him her bare ass and pussy.

A wave of control shimmered through him, but a moment later, the wolf took over, and the pain of his bones breaking and reforming, and his skin splitting to reveal his fur, fangs, and claws completely took him over.

Kiara spun and put her hands on her hips. "Well, you lasted a good three minutes that time. I guess that's an improvement."

"Only because I thought I was going to get to fuck you again when you showed me your wet cunt." He trotted over to her and stuck his nose directly between her legs, shifting back into his human form once again.

"As much as I like your cunt on my face, we'll have to save another ride on my beard for later. We have places to go and people to murder for interfering with our lives." He did give her cute little clit one quick kiss and a scrape of his teeth, as a promise for later.

"You are... both mean and delicious, and I love it. Now get out from between my legs so I can put my pants on." She stepped away but put one hand on his shoulder, both to keep him human and to support herself as she pulled her jeans on. "You better buy stock in some fancy plus-size underpants company if you're going to keep destroying all of mine. That's two pair in less than twenty-four hours."

"I think I used to own a kinkwear company back in Russia. Perhaps I can steal it back from Niko."

"Or you can ask him nicely when we get back to Rogue. I know you're sure he's a bad guy, but the Troikas have been really good to me, and I'd like if you would give them a chance. Why would Niko have your company anyway?"

Right. Shit. She didn't know. It was almost unfathomable that they were so deeply connected, and yet knew very little about each other's lives. He would fix that in the coming weeks, because he was planning on spending a lot of time just the two of them. Mostly in bed, but there had to be some pillow talk too. He didn't like that they had to start with the worst parts of his life. Although, honestly, his life as the Wolf Tzar wasn't exactly squeaky clean and shiny.

"The memories are all muddled in my brain from having been dragged through the Nothing to Hell and back by a whole host of demons, so I'm not completely sure, but Nikolai Troika assassinated me to take my throne."

"Your throne? Wait. You were the Wolf Tzar that everyone thought Niko killed? But he didn't. Those demons...." Kiara's eyes went wide and her mouth made an oh as she realized what she'd said. She covered her mouth with her hands and waited for him to make the same connection.

He was already there. In fact, he'd suspected that Rasputin had been working with demons. He was a power-hungry bastard. Being on the council that ruled over all of wolfkind wasn't enough for him, and Mik had always known that.

But he didn't expect his mentor, his advisor, to be the one to betray him. He hadn't expected his best friend either. so apparently, he wasn't a good judge of character.

"But in Niko's battle against the Volkovs they

exposed the demon, and he was just trying to use the wolves, to get them to side with them against the dragons." This all would have been nice to fucking know. He couldn't have, unless he'd wolfed up and actually confronted Niko. Instead he'd skulked around, stalking the Troikas and their mates, gleaning what little information he could.

He wasn't hiding in the shadows any longer. "It always comes back to those fucking dragons. You and I aren't here to do their bidding either."

She tapped her lip. "But what if they're the ones pulling all the strings? What if they've cursed us?"

"No, dragons don't have powers like that. Their magic is all elemental. Only Gods and Goddesses have the ability to mete out curses."

"See. One more thing the handbook would be good for. I'm making this happen if I have to write it myself. But surely the Goddess of the Moon wouldn't curse us and then ask us to help her just to reverse the curse, would she?"

He wouldn't put it past her. "Gods and Goddesses don't care about our lives or how they destroy them. However, the Goddess of the Moon did take care of her people long ago, so I don't know whether we can trust her or not. It does seem like an awfully long game if she cursed us thousands of years ago just to ask her favors now."

He wanted to believe the Goddess who created him and his people was good, but what other proof did he have since then. She hadn't exactly taken an interest in him until after he was murdered.

They weren't going to get to the bottom of this sitting in a castle in Prague contemplating conspiracies. "We need to go to where this all began."

"Umm, Sumer isn't a place anymore. So unless you know how to time travel, we're headed where?"

"Ancient Sumer was between the Euphrates and the Tigris, Mesopotamia. So, Iraq."

Kiara shook her head. "I don't even have a passport, and if I did, they aren't going to let a slightly unhinged American lady into Iraq anytime soon."

Right. He wasn't used to the restrictions normal humans, or even normal wolf shifters faced. He'd always been privileged. If he wanted to go somewhere, he went. That past was now his disadvantage. But he was no weak or stupid leader when he was the Wolf Tzar. He'd been misguided, but not dumb.

What else did they have at their disposal that he could use to keep his mate safe from the prying machinations of Gods and demons?

He could ask Eyrik and the wolf community here that his former guard trusted. He didn't like depending on others. Without his fortune and resources, he was going to have to figure out how to be something entirely new in order to survive.

He'd sprung his existence on Eyrik, and there were probably a few other guards who he'd trained, but most would likely be in Europe, not the Middle East. What they really needed were more contacts and connections. Other supernaturals who weren't under the influence of the Goddess.

"Kiara, who else do you know in the supernatural community, aside from the Troikas?" They were the last wolves he wanted to ask for help. "Perhaps someone you gave one of your predictions to?"

"That's mostly been other people around Rogue and some of them were humans..." Her words drifted off and she grabbed his hand. Her eyes didn't change and he didn't feel the telltale constriction in his chest, so it couldn't be a vision. "Something is coming."

The energy in the room shifted, almost buzzing around them. "Not something, someone."

Mik pushed Kiara behind him, putting her with her back against the wall. He took two steps forward and let the wolf rise up and take over, ready to eviscerate whoever was using the shadow to enter this realm.

Darkness grew in the corner adjacent to him, and he lowered his head, pooling the energy in his hind legs, ready to pounce the second they emerged. If it was demons or demon dragons, Kiara would have only moments to get away while he distracted them with his attack. *"Be ready to run."*

"Only if you're running too. Otherwise we're in this fight together." She ran to the other side of the room where the fireplace was set against the wall, boosted herself up onto a small ledge, and reached for a set of ancient, crossed swords hanging on the wall.

He didn't think they would budge, but they must have been hanging there for far too long, because the screws holding the rack encasing the swords pulled right out of the crumbling stone. She stumbled back with one sword in her hand, and the other clattered to the stone floor. "These things are heavier than they look."

She kicked the other one behind her and lifted her weapon of choice out in front of her like a tiny squire hefting her knight's enormous sword. She wasn't going to do anyone much harm unless she accidentally dropped the heavy metal on their toes. But if it made her feel safer and more secure, then that was half the battle.

The shadow shimmered. Whoever was using its portaling abilities was near. "*Get ready. Here they come.*"

But instead of an invading force of demons, one singular warrior woman, a sword of her own strapped to her back, popped out and fell to one knee in a bow before him."

"My Lord. I wondered when you and your consort would make an appearance in this lifetime. But your mating and awakening has sent ripples through the entire seven realms. By doing so you've put yourself and her in grave danger."

My Lord? This wasn't one of his people, nor a servant from his life as the Wolf Tzar. She was most definitely supernatural, but she wasn't a wolftress, or even a Goddess.

Kiara brought her sword point down and held it

directly in front of the warrior woman's face. "Who are you, and why should we trust you?"

The woman rose, pushed the sword gently away and glanced back and forth between him and Kiara. "The Cult of the Dead's dark magic grows stronger if your mating hasn't brought forth your memories. I am Ninshubar, servant to your daughter, my Lord, the Goddess Inanna. Your consort has a gift for her from her mother. I am here to retrieve it."

Ninshubar? Inanna?

Inanna, Goddess of Love and War.

Mik's heart skipped a beat, then another. His daughter.

But if Inanna was his daughter, and Ninshubar was here to retrieve the gift from the Goddess of the Moon, who was her mother... that meant, he'd sired children with the Goddess of the Moon.

What the actual fuck?

More importantly, who was this Cult of the Dead who was using their magic to keep him and Kiara from remembering who they were? This was exactly the kind of connection he needed to fuck up someone's life. Or afterlife.

This Ninshubar wasn't going anywhere until he had some answers. Like who the hell was he, truly. Because ancient Goddesses didn't have children with mere mortals, not even ones who were Tzars.

Mik turned and stared at Kiara. He hadn't actually spoken with the Goddess. He'd talked to Kiara, who was used by the Goddess to convey a message to him. Then later she'd gotten this gift of the spell from the Goddess as another task. But he hadn't seen the so-called woman who'd given it to her.

Was Kiara actually the Goddess of the Moon?

What did that make him?

FIND ME

Key didn't trust this Ninshubar. What kind of good guy popped out of shadows with swords? Nope. She was going to have to do better than that if she wanted the special Christmas ornament Taryn had given her. She was on a mission from a Goddess.

Oh, except she and Mik had decided the Goddess could take her mission and stuff it. Well, still. She wasn't handing over some fancy pants magic to just anyone. Someone out there in the supernatural world was trying to screw her out of having true love and until she found out who, no one was getting anything from her except for Mik.

If ever there was something to be angry about and let it all hang out it was this. Fuck whoever was messing with her love life... love lives.

The warrior woman pointed to the seashell Christmas

ornament Kiara wore around her neck. "Quickly, before the cult finds us all."

Mik growled and swished his tail all agitated-like. "*Don't give it to her, pchelka. There is something much more sinister going on here and we need more information from her. She knows our true identities.*"

Key gave Mik a quick nod and narrowed her eyes at the sword maiden from hell. "Excuse me, Ninsy-who-ha. But I don't know you from a hole in the wall, so forgive me if I'm not ready to just hand over a powerful spell from the Goddess of the Moon."

"Ninsy. I like that. You always were a tough cookie when it came to defending your God. That is something I can appreciate. Fine. I am willing to prove myself to you. Again." Ninshubar looked back at the shadow portal that hadn't closed behind her. "Hold your sword like I am, and aim for the bodies, not the shadows attached to them. Got it?"

"No. But okay." Shadows attached to bodies? That sounded like something out of a horror movie. Key did adjust her grip though. All the better to chop people's head off with. Especially if they were keeping secrets from her and Mik.

"And use your gift to anticipate their moves." Ninshubar squared up to the portal, putting herself between whatever danger was about to come through and the two of them. Either she was setting them up, or she really was on their side.

"I can do that?" She was getting pretty sick of not knowing anything about her so-called gift.

"Yes. Use the emotional connection you have with your mate." Ninshubar tipped her chin toward Mik. "His power is shared with you when you do that, and now that you're properly mated, you'll only grow stronger."

The Romani woman's warning that Key needed to complete the mating with Mik to fix her gift rang through her head again. Why did everyone else seem to know more about her, her powers, and her mate than she did? But fine. Key closed her eyes for a second and found that warm place behind her heart that she'd hidden away from the world. It was the very core of her being that she used to make it through life when things were too tough to carry on.

She'd found that same feeling when she was with him. He was her safe place to be who she truly was, the good and the bad, the woman and the witch. Key let that swirl around her chest and peeked one eye open to see if there were any visions floating about.

Nothing yet. "What about the curse or whatever it is that controls some of my visions?"

That took Ninshubar off guard. She jerked her head around and lowered her sword. "Someone else controls them? That's not supposed to—"

The rest of what she was about to reveal was cut off as the warmth moved from Key's chest to down between her legs. Key smiled for a second and mentally promised herself to reciprocate every filthy thing Mik had done to make her come.

In an uncomfortable flash, the room filled with a screech so bone-chilling, that Key actually trembled both in fear and from real cold. Her vision went a bit fuzzy around the edges and her chest tightened. Whatever was coming for them was a real monster. Probably with squishy tentacles and a face full of spider eyeballs or something equally horrifying.

So when a man in an expensive black suit and tie with ugly owls on it, wearing men-in-black style sunglasses, waltzed out of the shadowy portal, she forgot she was supposed to chop off his head with her thirteenth century sword.

Mik didn't. He attacked like the vicious beast that he was. He went for man-in-black, but a dead-eyed guy, also in a suit that looked like he'd been wearing it for about seven weeks straight, stepped between them. Blood splattered everywhere as Mik literally ripped the man's body from his head.

She'd seen the violence of the wolves before, of course she had, but Mik was something otherworldly. He wasn't a killing machine, he was a killing God. The more creepy, zombie-like men in black stepped out of the portal, the more he went berserk and either bit their heads off or sliced them to ribbons.

Ninshubar jumped into the fray immediately after Mik, and she wasn't half bad either. She was a master with that sword, and it appeared she wasn't afraid of zombie men in black who magically appeared out of dark portals either.

Key couldn't move. She tried to lift her sword and poke at the bad guys, but her muscles wouldn't respond. This felt very different to the regular fight or flight freeze up she experienced when danger was around. Did the man in black or the shadowy portal have some sort of magical control over her?

All she could do was stand there and watch Mik and Ninshubar fight. No, wait. There was a third person. Another woman with a sword just like hers. Had someone else joined their merry band of freaks and grabbed up the other sword she'd kicked behind her?

Perhaps the Goddess had come to their rescue. They could definitely use the help right about now. Especially if she brought her four big, bad guards with her.

But... this person's back was too familiar, the movements unskilled and awkward.

Oh shit. Shit, shit, shit, and more shit. A horrible hollow opened up in the very center of her chest as realization clawed its way out. That wasn't the Goddess of the Moon or any other freedom fighter.

Key was having a vision, one that she could actually see.

The other person fighting was her. The Kiara vision was fighting and losing the battle. Badly. Her other self tripped over her own sword and went headlong into Mik. A weird bleat of a squeal just popped out of vision Kiara's mouth, and they fell together, which caused Mik to shift back into his human form. His more fragile human form.

The main bad guy smiled down at the two of them, reached up for a shadowy figure floating around the top of his head, and directed it to attack. The thing screeched and dove along with the zombie guy it was attached to. The shadowy thing dove straight into Mik's chest, and he went from fighting and alive to still and dead in an instant.

He wasn't simply dead. That thing rose up out of him, dragging Mik's soul along with it.

Key couldn't react, she couldn't do anything but watch her entire world be taken from her in a moment. To the depths of her very being, she knew that if Mik's soul was taken by these monsters, he wouldn't be able to find her again in their next lives. He wouldn't have any more lives. He couldn't be reincarnated without a soul.

They would be separated forever.

She couldn't let that happen.

The zombie man in black grabbed the Kiara vision and shoved her toward the sunglasses wearing main man. "My Lord will be pleased with you."

Vision Kiara might as well be dead because she did nothing, completely shocked into a stupor by what had just happened. Sunglasses man dragged her away and the two of them disappeared into the shadowy portal. It closed like an angry asshole and the vision went black.

Key blinked, and the world around her went a little sideways. Her mouth opened of its own accord and words poured out of her. Instead of words, she began singing an old Credence Clearwater Revival song, but with slightly altered lyrics. The crazy words that went along with her vision poured out of her. "I see the Moon God rising. I see Chaos on the way. I see earth and hell combining. Find me in the next life. Don't go to Hell tonight. Even if they take your wife. The bad Moon God's on the way."

"Kiara, wake up. *Pchelka*, this is no time for a vision. Come back to me right now." Mik's voice rang through her head with an extra special spiciness to it.

She blinked again and she was looking up at Mik, wrapped in his arms. She could see Ninshubar out of the corner of her eye, in a fighting stance, her sword held aloft, ready to strike down whatever was coming through that portal.

But Key had already seen the man in black, the suited zombies, and the horrible killing shadows attached to them. They were going to kill Mik and take his soul. Not on her watch.

Key grabbed Mik's face and kissed him with everything she had. She filled her soul up with the flavor of him and his love for her. When she broke the kiss, he scowled at her, but also had the loveliest dark eyes that she would take the memory of wherever she was going.

She pushed away from him, grabbed the Christmas ornament from around her neck, and ripped it off. "Here, take this and give it to the red witch. That's what the Goddess, uh, my friend Taryn, said to do."

Key slapped the cord into Ninshubar's hand and then jumped directly in front of the portal. In the depths of the dark shadows, she saw the sunglasses man floating through, seconds from popping out.

"Kiara, no, what are you doing?" Mik jumped toward her, but it was too late.

A black suited arm wrapped around her and dragged her into a dark fog. She whispered, from her mind to Mik's as she was falling, falling, falling. "*Find me in the next life.*"

She heard no response. Her mind whirled around and around as if she was drunk, and pretty quickly her stomach revolted. If feeling like you were going to throw up while spinning in a thick dark fog was Hell, then she was in it.

An eternity and a half later, the dark fog parted, but was merely replaced by a slightly lighter grey area with no shape or form. She could be in a room, or she could be floating in space, she couldn't tell and, jeez, it was so hot here. The man in black was nowhere to be found. There was no one and nothing here.

"Hello, Priestess." The voice came from nowhere and everywhere all at once.

"Who you calling Priestess, punk?" Uh, not a punk at all. In front of her was man-sized birdcage with craggly black bars with an enormous, freaky-deaky looking owl inside.

"Welcome to the Nothing." The voice was coming from the owl. It wasn't moving its... beak, but the words weren't in her head like when Mik talked to her either. "Let me out of my cage and I'll send you back to your God, unharmed."

Why did she have the distinct feeling that he didn't mean God, as in the one in Heaven?

WITH A LITTLE HELP FROM
MY PACK

"Kiara, no!" Mik jumped toward the shadow portal and Kiara's fading form, but the portal closed with a whoosh so fast that it literally blew him back. He and Ninshubar were thrown against the stone wall of the castle.

He recovered first and clambered back to his feet. He had no time to waste recovering from injuries. He had to find a way to get to Kiara. Dread swirled around him, making his ears ring, and his blood buzz with rage. But also with fear.

There was very little that scared him in this life or any other he'd lived. Only one place struck fear into his heart. The shadow portal could lead to anywhere the practitioner of the element wanted it to go. But Mik had scented a very particular smell on that tainted human. The fire and brimstone of Hell.

If the demon-tainted human had taken here there, he

had to rescue her. Now. He was the one who should have surrendered and offered himself to save her, not the other way around. She was his savior, not a sacrifice.

He'd barely managed to escape after the demons had murdered him and dragged him down through the shadow into the underworld. Hell had tortured his soul so badly, he'd had to forsake his human form and retreat into his wolf or be destroyed.

Mere mortals didn't survive Hell. Not even with the help of Gods and Goddesses. Mortals didn't get murdered, exist in Hell, and escape. If he wasn't mortal, what was he, and why couldn't he remember? Who was fucking with him?

He didn't need to know right now. His only responsibility was sucking up his fears and going back to Hell if that's where she was.

Mik pinned Ninshubar in place with a menacing growl. *"You'll take me to her. Now."*

"My Lord, I cannot enter Hell." She bowed her head to him but shook it adamantly. "His minions are almost as dangerous as he is."

Fuck. He'd been right. That human with the taint of demons spread across his soul, had taken Kiara, his one true love and mate, to Hell. His worst nightmare.

Mik stalked toward the servant of Inanna, shifting back into his wolf form. It was something the world was going to have to get used to, because without Kiara, he was forevermore the Beast.

But he was also something more. Much, much more.

153

It wasn't Kiara who was an immortal, it was him. Mik's body filled with the power he'd long forgotten, and the world went dark. Night was his domain, and until he got his love back, darkness would prevail.

Ninshubar's eyes went wide, and she dropped down to one knee, her head bowed. But light filled the room once more. The light of the Moon. The light of the Goddess of the Moon.

His wife. Or the Goddess who once was his wife and mother of his children. He rounded on her and was faced with four wolves almost as big as he was, and a young woman dressed in jeans and a sweater with the Scottish lion and a unicorn emblazoned on it.

The wolves put themselves between him and Goddess Ningal.

"Sin, leave her be. Poor Ninshubar is a servant of Inanna's. She can't save your Priestess." Ningal waved her hand, and with a little pop and a spark of blue magic, the woman warrior was gone.

Sin. The Akkadian name of the God of the Moon. His name.

His. Name.

He was the God of the Moon.

"Bring her back. Or leave her be and you take me back to Hell, your choice. I will not allow Kiara to be tortured. I will burn down the fucking world to get to her, Ningal."

"We can't get into Hell. Not with our magic. Ereshkigal is playing a very long game and has enacted a spell to keep us out of this fight with her sister. Well, to keep me out of it. She didn't know about you. Her consort has done quite the gaslight job on her. Why we ever let the two of them get married is beyond me."

The more she talked of ancient times, the more memories filtered back to him. The light of her magic filled in holes in his mind. Ones that he didn't necessarily want to remember. "I don't recall letting anyone get married."

"No, I don't suppose you know much. It took me a year on the Island of the Damned and the love of four of my most faithful priests to bring my memories and magic back." She waved her hand about as if simply telling an interesting story, not talking about his fate and therefore the end of the world. "There are still some missing pieces here and there for me too."

"I don't give a fuck about your missing pieces. Who is doing this to me and how to I destroy them?"

Her wolves closed ranks around her and gave him warning growls. She ran her hands over each of their foreheads, calming them. "Ah, there's the vengeful God I know and don't love. Exactly who I've been wanting to show up."

"Why did you not simply tell me who I was before? Why fuck around with me first?"

"It doesn't work that way. You have to remember yourself, or there are catastrophic consequences. Remember Pompeii? Yeah, that was you, ya big whiner wolf. As it is I've probably told you too much, so don't be moving to California when this is all over, because you're likely to sink the whole place into the ocean or some-thing." Ningal poked him in the forehead right between his eyes.

"I know who I am." Mostly. He remembered that he was the God of the Moon, she was the Goddess of the Moon, they had some children who were giant pains in the asses. But not a whole lot else, like why or how he'd fallen in love with a mortal, or who wanted to keep him from her. "Now tell me who's cursed me?"

"Cursed us, dear husband. I've been living a thousand reincarnated lives trying to get back to my true loves too. He was very clever." She paced between her wolves. "I thought Ereshkigal had taken care of him, but I can see I was too lenient. I've been working my ass off trying to get you and Kiara back together so you would. Keep your rage directed at those that deserve it, and not me, buster."

"Dammit, Ningal. Who?"

"Taryn."

Yes. He would kill this Taryn, eat their remains, and shit them out. Good plan, but something was off. Taryn. Taryn? No, that didn't sound right. "Who the fuck is Taryn?"

"Me, asshole. Nobody has called me Ningal for like five thousand years. My name in this life is Taryn. Don't dead name me anymore. I only called you by your God name to give you a hint."

"Taryn, if you don't tell me who I need to erase from existence to get Kiara back, it will not only be your old name that is dead. I will tear through your guards and choke the information and the life out of you if you don't stop fucking with me right the hell now."

"Ooh, you always were a kinky bastard." Taryn wasn't even a tiny bit afraid of him and raised one eyebrow at him to show him so. "Think about it for a minute and quit expecting me to give you every damn bit of information. I told you it doesn't work that way, and I prefer not to live through a damn tsunami or some shit because I told you what you already know. Now think, douchepotato, think. Who's always been jealous that your daddy dearest gave us the night and the sky as our domain, and he got stuck in the underworld without any power to rule over it? Who covets any woman you've ever even looked at, much less loved?"

Only one other God could cause trouble like this. The God of Chaos. His jealous little brother. Fucking Nergal. "I'm going to kill him."

"Finally." Taryn grinned. "But you can't kill him."

"Watch me." It may take him another minute to remember how to destroy a god, but he would. He would tear Nergal into a thousand bite-sized pieces, and then send the bits of him across time and space so they could never be reunited.

Except for his cock.

That he was going to feed to a bunch of hungry birds just to make sure his asshole of a brother could never have any offspring of his own.

"I'd love to. But Ereshkigal locked him away in a cage in the Nothing, clever girl." Taryn tapped her temple.

"The second either of us enter it, we'll lose all our memories again and we won't have a clue why we're there."

The Nothing. The only thing worse than Hell. "How the fuck did he kidnap my mate then?"

"That I don't know. Obviously, he has some minions working for him. They call themselves the Cult of the Dead. Dumbasses. They don't have a clue how to worship a God." She made kissy faces and blew a kiss to her wolves.

The Cult of the Dead. Human. "I doubt they even know who they think they're worshipping. Probably the old human concept of the devil."

Humans he could kill. Had killed, and was about to kill some more.

But while he was an all-powerful god, he didn't have a clue how to use his powers, or if he even had any left. Thousands of years living as a wolf shifter hadn't helped. He wasn't going to be able to do this on his own, and he didn't want to rely on Taryn. She had her own priorities here and they didn't necessarily align with his.

He needed help from some old friends. Ones who were very good at tracking and taking down the bad guys. "Taryn, take me back to Rogue. I'm calling in an old debt."

"Oh. Fun. I'm gonna stop for popcorn on the way. I can't wait to see this." Taryn waved her hand, the stone room filled with her blue glowing magic, the stars and moon on the ceiling exploded, and Mik's brain blipped out.

In the next blink he was standing in an all too familiar forest, the light of the full moon dotting his fur as it filtered through the trees. The Reserve. He was back in Rogue.

Now to call in that favor.

He found the spot he was looking for, that crack in the earth filled with shadow. The portal to Hell. He lifted his face to the sky and howled. He howled for the lives he'd lived and lost, for the ache in his soul for his mate, and for every loyal friend who he thought had betrayed him to take his control and power.

Only one had betrayed him and it wasn't his oldest and best friend, Nikolai Troika.

The answering howls pierced the night. Mik stayed right where he was and waited for them to come to him. No more hiding in the shadows, no more misplaced anger, no need for any more subterfuge. He was here with an open heart and mind, hoping the most powerful mortal wolf would still be the same loyal and morally upright friend he'd spent so many years with.

The amber eyes of the Wolf Tzar's pure white wolf appeared first, followed by his brothers'. They approached cautiously, but without fear.

"You've finally come out of the shadows, Mikhail." Niko's alpha voice rang clear. Had Mik been an actual mortal wolf shifter, he would have felt its affects.

"Out of the shadows is apt. I have clawed my way out of hell, as I suspect you did too. But I'm here now to ask you to return with me."

Maxim and Konstantine lowered their heads and growled. Max stepped forward and put himself between Mik and Niko, protecting his Tzar. *"You won't be taking your thrown back by force, Mikhail Volkov."*

Mik gave a small tip of his head to Max but continued to address Niko. *"I'm glad that you have brothers so loyal to you. Not all of us are so lucky. But I'm not here for that. You are the rightful Wolf Tzar, and it suits both you and our people."*

Niko nudged Max and moved back to the point. *"What is it you want Mik, if not an alpha challenge?"*

"I'm here to ask for your help. My mate has been kidnapped, taken to Hell, and I..." He'd never had to admit this in his life, or any of his lives. He'd prided himself on being the leader of the pack, the biggest, best, and strongest wolf. But that hadn't helped him defeat his brother or kept him from losing Kiara over and over again. *"I am not powerful enough to rescue her on my own."*

"Your mate?"

"Yes. The one you know as Kiara Cross, the Oracle."

One more wolf loped into their circle. A wolftress, but an alpha in her own right. *"Key? You've mated with her? She is my responsibility, my pack. You should have talked to me first. But we can sort that out after we rescue her. Let's rally the troops. Where to?"*

Mik liked this wolftress and if she was friends with Kiara, he was looking forward to having her around.

"There is an entrance to Hell, right here in your Reserve. It will be a perilous journey, and—"

The crack in the earth and stone creaked and shadow bubbled out of it. A portal was opening right before their eyes. Nergal must be sending more of his Cult to disrupt Mik's plans. He placed himself directly in the line of fire where the demons or the Cult would emerge, ready to destroy anyone that dared to interfere with the rescue of his mate.

No demon or tainted human popped out of the portal. Kiara did.

She took one step forward, threw her arms around his neck, shifting him instantly into his human form, and then collapsed into his arms.

I WILL ALWAYS FIND YOU

*W*olves, and people, and friends, and her lover were hustling, bustling, and fussing over her. She recognized the voices and the love from Max and Gal, Poppy and Harley, Kosta and Heli, Niko and Zara, and even Taryn and her four mates.

Was she being a little overdramatic? Yes.

Would she do it again? Also yes.

For the first time in... maybe ever, it was really damn nice to be the center of attention. She was going to milk it for all it was worth. But first she was going to make sure Mik was okay and that he knew she was too. She kept her eyes closed but reached out to him with her mind.

"I'm okay, Mikhail. Just tired. Hell is really far away, and it took pretty much everything I had to get out."

"My love, my love. Don't ever do that to me again. I was scared to death over you."

Aww. Her big bad wolf just admitted that he was

scared. She'd done that to him. While she was going to enjoy the hell out of this tender moment between them, she looked forward to getting her big grumpy, growly mate back soon.

"I think the entire town and maybe a couple of neighboring ones have come out to help and make sure you're okay."

It was really nice and cool that they all showed up for her. She normally didn't like everyone to fuss over her, but she'd decided that sometimes, it was okay to let others take care of you for a little bit. She'd been alone for so long, so many lifetimes, that this time, now that she had Mik back, she wasn't letting any love out of her life, and she was going to be truly grateful for all that she had.

The real kind of grateful this time. If this experience had taught her anything it was the difference between fake gratitude to make yourself feel better and the soul deep thankfulness of having people around who really cared about you and who meant the world and more to you.

"I guess I'll open my eyes and tell them I'm okay too."

"Yes. Do that, and quickly, because I need you with all that I have." Mik brushed a kiss over her forehead. "We are going to spend a very long time proving how alive we are to each other. Days. Weeks. I'm going to be inside of you until I can breath again because I know you're alive and well."

Key opened her eyes and looked up at the love of a thousand lives. "I think you said that last part out loud."

She glanced at the group of friends standing closest to

them and yep, their mouths were all hanging open. Poppy was the first to recover. "Awww. I love hanging around the newly mated. Remember when we couldn't keep our hands off each other either, Harley? "

"You mean this morning, *meelaya moy*?" Harley smiled and pulled Poppy in for a not so quick kiss.

Key tried to get up, but Mik did not let her go. Okay, then. She didn't want to be very far away from him either. Not after everything she'd learned while hanging out with a Christmas ornament collecting witch in Hell. Instead she wrapped her arms around his neck and just sat more upright in his arms so she could talk to her friends properly.

She knew the question was coming but she didn't expect Taryn to be the first to ask, or so bluntly.

"So, Key, how was Hell and how did you escape?" The way she said it was all sing-songy, more like an old friend asking for gossip.

But all eyes, including Mik's, turned to her for the answer. "I was about to mount a rescue mission to come and get you."

"Thanks, but I saved myself. Mostly. I'm glad you didn't have to. No one should spend any more time than absolutely necessary in that place." She shivered, although it would have been more apt to fan herself. Hell was hella hot. "It's the worst and really does smell like rotten eggs and, weirdly, lizard pee."

Mik grumbled. "*Pchelka*, how did you escape?"

Oh, right. They probably did want to know all about

that. "So, I was stuck talking to this horrible owl who would not shut up about being stuck in a cage. I didn't like him at all, and decided to just walk away. That really pissed him off, but what was he going to do, he was locked up."

"You walked away from the God of Chaos?" Mik asked the question, but his mouth stayed hanging open. Key reached up and shut it for him.

"He never said who he was. Then I met this absolutely batshit crazy woman who said I didn't belong there. Like, she was mad about it. Kept saying her mother never said anything about me and that I needed to leave because she was very busy with a mermaid at the moment and didn't have time for me."

Taryn clapped her hands. "Fuck yeah, she did. That's my girl."

Hold up. "You know her?"

Taryn made a moue and rolled her eyes. "Who do you think I sent the spell to?"

Oh my God. That made so much sense now. But if crazy lady was the red witch, Key did not want to stick around to see how she was going to use that spell.

Except, she didn't have to wait to find out. She could use her power now if she wanted to know. But... maybe later. She'd rather use her psychic abilities to see how down and dirty she and Mik were going to get when everyone else left and they were blissfully alone.

Mik growled at Taryn and held Key tighter. "All right, as you can see, my mate is fine. I'm sure she'll share much more of the details of her story later. I thank you all for coming to help, but we would like some privacy."

No one paid any attention to him at all. Key snuggled into his chest and said, "Sweetheart, bring out a little of that big bad wolf I love so much."

Mik kissed the top of her head, and she felt the rumble in his chest before she heard the growl. Man, oh man what it growl it was. Delicious. "Get the hell out of my mate's house so I can fuck her brains out. Now."

The room cleared out real quick of everyone except for Taryn and her mates. "I have just a couple more things before we go."

Mik snarled. "Fine, but be quick about it."

Taryn gave him a look and Key returned it to her. Nobody was allowed to give Mik shit except for her. She motioned to Taryn to get on with it.

"Key, do you have your memories back?"

She shrugged. "I don't know how to answer that. How would I know?"

"You would know and that's very strange. I'm not sure Nergal's curse over you two is completely broken and I think that could mean mine isn't either. We all need to be careful and keep in touch about anything strange that happens."

"Just because you're my Goddess wife, doesn't mean we have to be friendly, Taryn. Go away now, and let me be with my true love."

Excusie-what-now? Key grabbed Mik's chin and brought his face down to hers. "She's your wife? I'm the other woman? Nope. No. Don't like that. You two are getting a divorce right now."

Taryn laughed. "Don't be so old fashioned. We aren't bound by any Earthly laws. We united because we thought we were supposed to. Our immortal family is an incestuous shitshow. Why do you think we both sought out other lovers? I my found true love with my priests, and you," she pointed to Mik, "with your priestess. Let's leave it at that."

Ah. That's why the owl called her a priestess. Interesting. "Okay, fine. I'll forgive you if you invite us to dinner and tell me the rest of that story. In like a week."

Mik grunted. "Make it a month."

Taryn nodded. "Fine. I'll tell her, but I'm not telling you. See if you can't remember before then. I like my seaside hotel where it is."

"What?"

"Apparently, if she tells me anything about my true identity, I cause natural disasters, but if I figure it out on my own, then all is right with the world."

Huh. "Did you remember who we are?"

"Partly. It's still sketchy and I don't think you're going to believe it."

Fun. "Tell me in bed. I'm exhausted." She looked over at Taryn. "Hint, hint."

"Yep, we're going. See you next month, unless you get anymore visits from the Cult of the Dead or you remember who you are. Then we can kick it and talk about old times. Probably don't mention it to anyone else though. People freak out when they find out they're living next door to legends of mythology." Taryn waved her hand and she and her guards disappeared in a blip of blue moonlight.

"Taryn really is the Goddess of the Moon, isn't she?"

"Yes, love. But enough about her. Please strip right here and now so that I can check every bit of your body for injuries."

There was something special in the way he liked her to take off her clothes for him, and then how he worshipped her body once she did.

A white fog rolled across her vision, but Key pushed it away and let the vision form unhindered. She was once again in that ancient temple, but alone. She was standing before the altar of Sin, the God of the Moon, and she was removing her clothes just like she did for Mik.

The carving of the moon and stars on the stone altar lit up and flashed so bright, it was if the moon was the sun for a brief moment. But then, standing there in front of her was Sin, in the flesh.

The God cupped her face, bringing her genuflected chin up. "You worship me, my little bee, but I am here to worship you and your body. Give yourself to me."

The love in this God's heart flowed from his fingers to her and when she looked into his face, she saw not only him, but the face of a thousand lovers, including Mik. Each and every one of them was him. They were all the God of the Moon, her love, the love of a thousand lifetimes.

Key let the vision go and looked up into that same face. The face of a God who loved her, who found her in every lifetime, and who fought for her in each of them. A God that she would claim as her own forever, who she would always love.

WHAT'S up with those dragons?

Want to see what happened to the wedding planner who was kidnapped by that green dragon warrior?

Read Chase Me: Dragons Love Curves book one now!

EXCERPT FROM CHASE ME

CHAPTER 1: ALWAYS THE WEDDING PLANNER, NEVER THE BRIDE

*A*gh. Ciara's feet ached, her back was stiff and the headache she'd staved off with some ibuprofen four hours ago was rapidly creeping back behind her left eyeball. Nothing like the sweet pains of victory.

One more commission like this and she could afford to take that beach vacation she'd been promising Wesley for the past three years.

"Oh Sarah, there you are." The bride's mother, who was reason number one, two, three, and forty-three for said headache, waved her over. Mother-of-the-Bridezilla paid the bills, so Ciara pasted on her most helpful smile and greeted the table.

"Hello everyone. Having a nice time?"

Headache mom turned to the couple sitting next to her. "Bill, Thi, this is Sarah, the wedding planner. You simply must book her for your Linh's wedding. She is the best—always available for her clients. I called her last week at two in the morning when I simply knew that Bethany needed to have three more wedding cakes at the reception. Sarah never says no."

Oh, great. That's what she wanted to be known for. Being the slut of the wedding planner world.

"Well, I like to hear that. We want our baby to have everything she wants for her wedding. No expense spared. Do you have a card, Sarah?"

"It's Ciara actually, and yes, of course." She handed Bill, who she could already tell was wrapped around his daughter's little finger, a card. Bill handed the card to his wife. "Let me write your time and date on the back for you."

She pulled a pen out of her kit. Always prepared, true to her Girl Scout roots. She scribbled on the back of the card.

"Ciara Mosley-Willingham. Do you own Willingham Weddings, dear?"

Sigh. Not yet. Not ever if her mother had anything to do with it. "That honor goes to my mother, Wilhelmina."

"Ah, I see. Well, nepotism has its benefits." The table all chuckled at Bill's little joke.

Benefits schmenefits. If only they knew.

"I've got an appointment that just opened up for two weeks from Monday. Will that work to bring Linh in for a consultation?"

"Two weeks?"

She nodded. "I'm afraid the next available is in August."

The couple glanced at each other. They were not used to waiting patiently. Most of her clients weren't.

"That's almost three months from now."

Headache mother raised a glass of champagne. "You wanted the best. Better get her while you can."

Thi raised an eyebrow, trying to intimidate Ciara. Not gonna happen. Ciara gave the mother her award-winning account-getting smile.

Thi gave in. "We'll be there."

Bali with Wesley, here she comes. If she could ever get him to ask her out in the first place, and in another three years when her schedule cleared up. Not that her mother would ever allow her to take a vacation, but at least now she had a plan to get that date with the hunk of the office.

Ciara made her rounds, vying for a chance to run into Wes with the good news. News that should be celebrated, with a night on the town, a nice dinner, some satin sheets.

She checked in with the catering staff and found out he was in the kitchen. Wes, in a perfect three-piece suit with the purple pocket square and matching vest, just about took her breath away. How any man this good looking would be interested in her blew her mind.

By interested, she meant he flirted with her constantly at the office but hadn't ever asked her out. Ciara had made it perfectly clear she was willing and available.

He hinted, she smiled and nodded, and then nothing.

A girl could only wait so long for the man of her day dreams to make a move.

"Hey babe." He kissed her on the cheeks while holding his cell phone to his ear. "We've got a champagne shortage crisis on our hands."

No need to stress. Cool, calm, and collected. Always. "No problem. I'll bring in the secret back-up case I keep in my car."

Wes hung up his phone and winked at the disheveled waiter with the empty tray. "Told you Ciara would swing some of her magic."

He was such a sweet talker. She hoped he was a dirty talker too. Whoa, wait. Down girl. She had to get a date with him first. "I'll go grab it, but the bouquet toss is in a few minutes. Go chat up all the single girls and talk them into standing up to catch the bouquet."

One wink or an eyebrow waggle from him and they'd all be smashing each other in the face to catch those flowers whether they wanted to or not.

"I'll go get the champagne, you go catch the bouquet." Wes shook his head and shivered.

Lots of bouquets were in her future, but not for catching. Always the wedding planner, never the bride. Yet.

Here goes nothing, or something, or gah, just ask him.

"Hey, I just landed the Barton wedding. We should celebrate."

Wes grinned. "You are going to make us all zillionaires. I cannot even keep up."

Okay, this was going well. Ask him. "So, you'll go out with me to celebrate?"

"You bet."

He didn't hesitate even a little. She should have asked him months and months... and months ago.

"Are you free on Wednesday?" They had weddings on the weekends, but she hoped she didn't sound lame for suggesting a weeknight.

"Nope. But, I could do Thursday. Dinner, drinks, and I know the greatest place to go clubbing."

Dinner, drinks, and dancing. Perfect.

She wanted to jump up and down and clap her hands.

Not appropriate.

Be cool.

Ciara drew upon her inner cucumber-ness. "Sounds great."

Enough said. Right? Yeah, that was fine. She didn't want to look overly enthusiastic. She'd save that for the in-bed portion of their evening.

Geez, she needed to get her mind out of the gutter. She'd gone from dinner and dancing to handcuffs and blindfolds in seconds. Oh, please let him be at least a little kinky.

"Ciara?"

"Yeah?" She blinked, still caught up in her fantasy sex life with Wesley.

"You feeling alright? You look a little flushed."

She'd be fine and dandy if she could get the real Wesley into her fantasy life. "Yep. Great. Go grab that champagne and get it on ice."

"You're the best, you know that, right?" Wes grabbed her in a bear hug and danced her around. He jerked back and rubbed at his chest. "Ouch, your necklace bit me."

"Oh, geez. Sorry." Ciara put her hand over the colorful pendant she'd gotten a few days ago. She didn't feel anything sharp.

"Pretty but painful, doll." Wes examined the charm, staring a scant inch above Ciara's boobs. "It would go with everything. Where'd you get it?"

Damn. She'd kind of hoped Wesley had sent it. Not likely, but she was ever hopeful. Must be from her mother, who rarely gave gifts. Weird.

"Oh my god, Ciara, there you are. I'm getting a divorce, or is it an annulment? Whatever. George is such an ass. I want out of this marriage right now." The bride ran into the kitchen and faux collapsed into Ciara's arms.

She glanced at Wes, who shook his head and smirked. He mouthed the words good luck and backed away from them.

This woman wasn't the first newlywed to freak out at the reception and she wouldn't be the last. Ciara had a long track-record of calming them down and helping them focus on what was important, their happily ever afters. Wesley called her the bride whisperer.

Ciara put a hand on the bride's arm and sent all the happy calming positive thoughts she could muster. They took a deep breath together.

"You can do this. Everything is going to be fine."

The bride nodded, looking a little dazed and repeated Ciara's words. "Everything is going to be fine."

A few hours later, the bride and groom had more than made up. The bouquet was tossed, the champagne chilled and toasted, the candles blown out, all topped off by the perfect sunset.

At two in the morning, Wes escorted the last of the drunken groomsmen to the limos they'd arranged to drive the non-sober home and Ciara collapsed into the nearest chair.

If she took her shoes off now, they were never ever going back on, but she'd limp home barefoot rather than take one more second in her not-so-high heels.

A lonely uneaten piece of wedding cake had been calling to her ever since she saw the fit groomsman walk away from it several hours ago. After that marathon wedding and reception, she needed a good sugar fix.

"Stop right there, thief." The deep rumble of a male voice halted the fork midway to her mouth. Sounded like he was back for his dessert. Oh God. How embarrassing.

"I'm just doing a bit of quality control. Have to make sure the cake is up to Willingham Weddings standards."

Please don't let him mention the fact that the wedding

was over. Ciara turned to give the groomsman her best don't mind me I'm just the chubby, dateless, wedding planner stealing a piece of leftover cake smile. The man-slash-movie-star-slash-romance novel cover model standing three feet behind her had his arms crossed and a mad as hell glare on.

He wore a tight black t-shirt, dark jeans and a beautiful bright green crystal on a cord around his neck, so he wasn't the groomsman, or any other guest of the Ketcher-Fast wedding. She'd remember all that fantasy material.

He glanced down at the glowing charm at his throat and stilled. He faltered for a second and had to grab on to a chair to keep his balance.

Great. Another drunk guest and all the limos were gone. No way was she driving him home herself. Hmm. Well, maybe. He was awfully sexy and all those daydreams she'd had about Wes all night suddenly starred this magnetic stranger.

Until he growled at her. "I don't give a damn about the cake, unless that is where you've hidden my goods."

"Your goods?" The only goods Ciara could comprehend at the moment were six, or maybe eight, of the most beautifully defined abdominal muscles in the whole Four Corners.

He crossed the scant yard between them in two strides, hauled her up out of the chair, and got so far into her personal space bubble she could smell his cinnamony breath. A zing whipped through her from every place he touched and strangely, she really wanted to stand up on her tippy toes and press her lips to his, taste that spice, lick up every essence of that erotic flavor.

She might have too if he'd held her for a second longer. But, after searching her eyes, he released her and began pacing, prowling around her, his eyes roving her from head to toe.

He might have the body of a god and she the body of a cupcake, but she would not be intimidated by wandering eyes. "First of all, you have to tell me what brand of toothpaste you use, and second, back up out of my business, buster."

"Do not try to beguile me with your talk of hygiene products, your hair of gold, and your body made for sin. Where have you hidden my Wyr relic, witch?" He stopped circling and stared straight at her butt.

Body made for sin? Was he kidding? Body made of sins, maybe. Namely the sins of Swiss meringue buttercream, chocolate ganache, and too many I Love Lucy reruns. "Stop staring at my tuchis. Whatever you're looking for ain't in there."

She wiggled her backside to emphasize her point. That made her intruder damn irritated, probably that her rear wasn't dropping any evidence of wrong doing based on the growl rumbling from his chest and his eyes glued to her ass.

"Stop enticing me with your curves, thief. You cannot distract me from what is mine."

Ciara cleared her throat, gently at first, but when that

failed to bring his eyes up to hers, she about gave herself a sore throat trying to get his attention.

"Are you ill? I won't have you dying before you tell me where the statue is hidden."

What an asshat. A cute one, but a real douche canoe nonetheless. "I think maybe we've gotten off on the wrong foot here." Ciara extended her hand to him. "I'm Ciara Mosley-Willingham." Her hand hung there for a full count of ten. "And you are?"

He recoiled from her hand. "Wondering what kind of spell you're trying to work on me. Whatever it is, I assure you a Wyvern is immune."

"I was trying to be nice, but I've had a very long and tiring day, so my patience is wearing thin. I don't have your thingy, and I don't know what a why Vern is. I thought for a minute I might help you try to find it, but I'm done now." Ciara turned and began looking for her torturous heels. It would be much more fun to stomp off if there was some clack.

"As am I. If you won't return what you have taken from me I will be forced to bring you before the AllWyr council."

"What the hell?"

He grabbed her hand and pulled her through the ball-room toward a terrace. Good thing she'd already kicked off her shoes or she'd have been tripping all over her feet at the rate he was dragging her away.

"Hey, stop right this instant or I'll bring out the self-defense moves."

"Save your defense for the council. You'll need it."

This dude was seriously a wackadoo. Where was the pepper spray when she needed it? Oh, that's right, still in the bag from the store her mother had insisted they buy in bulk from.

"Let me go."

"Return my relic."

"I'm gonna make you a relic."

"Save your spells, witch."

"Your face is a witch."

The scary man released her and grabbed at his face. When he didn't find anything wrong with it, he narrowed his eyes and glared at her. "Good try, witch. You'll pay for that."

Ciara pivoted and bolted weaving her way between the tables. One second she was zigging and zagging, the next she was airborne.

Great talons gripped her shoulders and a deep whoosh-whoosh-whoosh sounded above her.

She wriggled and screamed, frantically trying to see what was happening above her. Her feet crashed into empty glasses and caught a centerpiece of giant lilies dead-on as she was dragged through the air above the tables.

Before she could even take another breath to scream again, they swooped out of the French doors, over the balcony and into the night sky.

Ciara lost her effing mind as the ground beneath her sunk down into tiny squares of land. She couldn't look any longer, or she'd throw up. So instead she glanced up, not fathoming that she'd see flying above her the giant wings, flapping gracefully through the sky, of a dragon.

JOIN in Ciara's adventures with her Dragon Warrior Jakob in Chase Me

ACKNOWLEDGMENTS

Great big thanks to my Mushrooms - JL Madore, Claudia Burgoa, Dylann Crush, M. Guida, and Bri Blackwood. I appreciate all your help and patience as I burn hard.

I'm so grateful for my Amazeballs Writers - Danielle Hart, Stephanie Harrell, Davina Storm, and Cara Bryant who are always willing to get on and do writing sprints with me. I appreciate it more than you could know, and am infinitely proud of your successes in publishing.

My Amazeballs Facebook group is so much of the reason I keep writing and I look forward to logging onto the FaceSpace every day and seeing what kind of fun and games we've got going on!

Big thanks to my proofreader, Chrisandra. She probably hates commas as much as I do now. All the remaining errors are all my fault. I'm sure I screwed it up somewhere.

I'm ever grateful to Elli Zafiris and Becca Syme for telling me I'm worth fighting for when I'm sure I've effed up my book and my career. You two are my energy pennies.

I am so very grateful to have readers who will join my on my crazy book adventures where there will ALWAYS be curvy girls getting happy ever afters!

Without all of you, I wouldn't be able to feed my cats (or live the dream of a creative life!)

———

Thank you so much to all my Patreon Book Dragons!

An enormous thanks to my Official Biggest Fans Ever. You're the best book dragons a curvy girl author could ask for~

Thank you so much for all your undying devotion for me and the characters I write. You keep me writing (almost) every day.

Hugs and Kisses and Signed Books and Swag for you from me! I am so incredibly grateful for each of you and am awed by your support.

- Helena E.
- Alida H.
- Daphine G.
- Bridget M.
- Stephanie F.
- Danielle T.
- Marea H.
- Marilyn C.
- Mari G.
- Cherie S.

- Jessica W.
- Katherine M.
- Kelli W.

Shout out to my Official VIP Fans!
Extra Hugs and to you ~

- Jeanette M.
- Kerrie M.
- Michele C.
- Corinne A.
- Deborah S.
- Frania G.
- Jennifer B.
- Hannah P.
- Janice M.
- Nicole W.
- Sandra B.
- Sherrie W.
- DebbieJoy G.
- Heather R.
- Janice W.
- Robin O.

Dragons Love Curves

Chase Me

Tease Me

Unmask Me

Bite Me

Cage Me

Baby Me

Defy Me

Surprise Me

Dirty Dragon

Crave Me

Dragon Love Letters - Curvy Connection Exclusive

Slay Me

Play Me

The Black Dragon Brotherhood

Tamed

Tangled

Twisted

Fated For Curves

A Touch of Fate

A Tangled Fate

A Twist of Fate

Alpha Wolves Want Curves

Dirty Wolf

Naughty Wolf

Kinky Wolf

Hungry Wolf

Grumpy Wolves

Filthy Wolf

The Fate of the Wolf Guard

Unclaimed

Untamed

Undone

Undefeated

Claimed by the Seven Realms

Protected

Stolen

Crowned

By Aidy Award and Piper Fox

Big Wolf on Campus

Cocky Jock Wolf

Bad Boy Wolf

Heart Throb Wolf

Hot Shot Wolf

Contemporary Romance by Aidy Award

The Curvy Love Series

Curvy Diversion

Curvy Temptation

Curvy Persuasion

The Curvy Seduction Saga

Rebound

Rebellion

Reignite

Rejoice

Revel

ABOUT THE AUTHOR

Aidy Award is a curvy girl who kind of has a thing for stormtroopers. She's also the author of the popular Curvy Love series and the hot new Dragons Love Curves series.

She writes curvy girl erotic romance, about real love, and dirty fun, with happy ever afters because every woman deserves great sex and even better romance, no matter her size, shape, or what the scale says.

Read the delicious tales of hot heroes and curvy heroines come to life under the covers and between the pages of Aidy's books. Then let her know because she really does want to hear from her readers.

Connect with Aidy on her website. www.AidyAward.com get her Curvy Connection, and join her Facebook Group - Aidy's Amazeballs.

Made in United States
Troutdale, OR
04/11/2024

19124980R00127